Dedication: *To Christi; my wife, soul mate, and best friend, whose love inspired me to write this kind of story. Spending time watching some of those romance movies with her while I was playing Texas Hold 'Em on my phone app gave me the idea for this book. To our children Anastasia, Kosta, and Shannon, the rewards in our life; To them; we hope and pray for the greatest blessings life has to offer.*

PROLOGUE: *This is a fictional romantic comedy story about two people finding true love in a most unusual set of circumstances. Danny, a young widower and father of two begins his search for a new soul mate to share his life. Since he married his high school sweetheart he never really dated before. Actually dating for the first time was an eye opener for him as he finds himself in all kinds of situations that are shocking and strange to him. Christy, a young widow and mother of one, seeks the same. They encounter many situations that go awry where the people they meet turn out to be anything but right for them. After years of frustrating and humorous encounters they temporarily put their search on hold to take a much needed break. Their chance meeting while playing an online game of Texas Hold 'em poker brought them together despite living miles apart and keeping their identities a secret from one another. You'll laugh and cheer at this heartwarming story of how two lonely people find each other.*

The King & Queen of

Hearts: A Texas Hold 'em Romantic Comedy

by Dennis C Mariotis

U.S. Copyright Registration # TX 8-522-827

April 27, 2018

Disclaimer: This book is a work of fiction. Names, characters, businesses, places, events and incidents are either the products of the author's imagination or used in a fictitious manner. Any resemblance to actual persons, living or dead, or actual events is purely coincidental.

Photo on Cover & Last Page: It's a picture of the actual wedding crowns worn by the author Dennis and his wife Christi during their wedding ceremony where they were crowned King & Queen of their home. The crowns are kept in a picture box hanging in their home as a keepsake. As for the two cards? Well for that you'll have to enjoy the book! Photo on back cover taken by Anastasia Mariotis.

To the reader from the Author: *It takes a lot of time, commitment, effort, cost, research, and proofing to write a book. For this I kindly request and will very much appreciate you to take a minute of your valuable time and give this book a good rating on Amazon.com books. This helps other sites such as Ebay, Books-A-Million, Barnes & Noble, etc. pick up and list the book on their sites. I hope you enjoy the story. Thank you,* Dennis C Mariotis

Chapter 1
The Widower

"**All** *in!" Chris said. Without changing his expression, Danny peaked at his hole cards, then looked up at Chris and studied his face for about fifteen seconds. Counting out his chips to 'call' the bet, Danny moved them into the pot. "Call. And I do believe I have you beat," said Danny. Flipping his hole cards over Chris responded, "Not with three-of-a-kind. Read 'em dad...Trip Aces! Wooo hooo!" Breaking his poker-face Danny smiled and said, "Nice! Very good! But not good enough." Turning his hole cards over Danny's smile grew larger as he said, "Full house. Deuces over aces! Read 'em son!" Chris sat back, folding his hands across his chest and shaking his head he asked, "How do you do that? How do you put on such a poker-face? I can't read you for the life of me! No wonder why your poker buddies don't like to play with you. I could swear you looked like you were beaten!"*

Danny sat with a stoic stare at Chris. Then, breaking the blank stare he said, "You mean this face?" Chris smiled and answered, "Yeah dad. That face. *Do you practice in front of a mirror, or do you have an acting coach?*" Breaking his blank look Danny smiled and said, "I used to play a lot of poker with your mother, and she was able to read my cards like my face was a mirror. I couldn't hide my hand from her. She would tell me what my cards were when I made certain facial expressions, or breathed too deep, or shallow, or swallowed, or blinked. And every time, she beat me like a red-headed step-child. So I began to practice changing my expressions when we played. But she was too good. One day she said to me: 'Honey! You're trying too hard and it's not working.' She got so tired of beating me, that she coached me on how to keep an 'un-readable' look on my face no matter what my hand was. She shuffled the deck, then rearranged the cards so I would be dealt either four aces, or a royal flush, or a pair, or absolutely nothing. With each different hand, she closely watched my every expression. When I finally held the same 'poker-face' for ten straight hands, she told me that was the one I needed to keep and always use it. After that, I used that same facial expression every time I played anything. Later, I learned how to change my expressions to fake out my opponents. Then I began to be real competition for her. From then on, the games became fun for both of us. Since then, I learned to read peoples' faces, and I became better at being able to tell *what kind of hand they held. Mostly by reading their eyes. Just like that country song about playing poker. I knew when to stay in, and when to get out. Mom was better than me at this so she taught me all the things about playing poker that she knew. She told me her grandpa taught her how to play, and how to read her opponents. That's just another one of the many things I really miss about her!" Chris looked down and said, "Yeah. Me too. She was a great mom. And now I know why she always beat me and sis at these games." They shared a good laugh at Chris' comment.*

"Well, it's getting late and Donna is probably asleep by now," said Chris. "You've got a good lady by your side son. Keep her happy," responded Danny. "She's a good wife dad, and knows how much the time we have together means to me, and she doesn't mind at all. But, she's really concerned about you, dad," Chris said as he stood up and put on his jacket. Danny replied, "I know. I know. She's concerned that I've been alone way too long, and wants me to find someone soon. She's a great daughter-in-law and I appreciate her worrying about me. Give her a hug and tell her 'thanks and I love her.' But also tell her I'm doing fine. It's been two years since your mom died and I haven't found anyone yet. And I'm surely NOT going to settle for someone just to have company. I've been out a couple of times and so far, nothing feels right. I'll keep trying, but give me some time. It's not easy.

I want to find a good friend first. Then, if it feels right between us, we'll take it to the next level. I'd rather be alone, than to be with someone I jumped into a relationship with too quickly, then only to find out it's a bad match. **Noooo thank you!"** *Opening the front door Chris turned and gave his dad a hug and told him, "Good night. Love you dad." Danny replied, "I love you too son. Drive home carefully. The weatherman's calling for some pretty rough thunderstorms and high winds tonight." Chris nodded as he walked out the door to his car. Unlocking it, he got in, cranked it up, and drove off. Danny watched his son's car leave the driveway before closing and locking the front door.*

Walking into the kitchen to get a glass of water, Danny stopped and looked around the room. He stood there in the silence thinking about his wife Rachel, and how they held hands every night as they walked upstairs to their bedroom to retire for the evening. Some nights, shortly after Rachel passed away, Danny would imagine she was walking with him hand-in-hand up the stairs. At this point though, Danny was well past that imaginative walk. Now when he reached the bedroom he would lie down on the bed, and reminisce about his life with his beautiful wife before he fell asleep. Most of the time he laid in bed and relived many special moments with her. Tonight, lying there, his thoughts were of how twenty-

seven years of marriage flew by so quickly. Then he thought way back to the beginning of their relationship.

They were high school sweethearts who married as soon as they turned eighteen. He winced at the thought of how they struggled to make ends meet. Then he smiled as he thought about how he couldn't believe how in the world they both made it through college, while working every minute they could to pay for rent; put food on the table; gas and insurance for their jalopy; and manage to pay for college tuition and books. Then he shivered at the thought of how they were able to pay off the hospital bills, as well as, raise and support twins in their first year of marriage. They would have either filed for bankruptcy or quit college if it wasn't for both of their parents pitching in to help babysit their children. Daycare expenses were astronomical and unaffordable even if they were both working full-time, let alone him working part-time, and Rachel working full-time until he received his degree. After he graduated, Danny landed a full-time job that paid well, and had great benefits. Then it was Rachel's turn to go to college. By that time their kids were in school and after-school day care was very affordable.

He reminisced about his two children when they were newborns, and, despite their financial struggles, he thought about all the fun and wild times they had raising Chris and Vicky, as he and Rachel were barely adults themselves. He laughed out loud thinking about the times he changed 'poopy-diapers', and how he heaved and gagged every time without fail. Rachel never gave in though, no matter how much he coughed, choked, and carried on during the process. She made him take his turn and it never failed to make her laugh so hard every time he unsuccessfully tried not to let the messy and smelly diaper bother him. She even took pictures of his 'disgusted' facial expressions, and placed them in their family albums. Before he turned out the light he smiled and thought of how fortunate he was for those memories, and never had a single regret about anything. Those were times he would not change for anything in the world.

Falling asleep almost always took time for Danny. He tossed and turned sometimes for hours. Occasionally during the night, he would close his eyes, and reach across the bed hoping his arm would come to rest across Rachel's body. Feeling only the bedspread, he opened his eyes and sighed from the disappointment of the vacancy in the space next to him. Two years since Rachel passed away, and he cringed at the thought of how his habits continued, even in his sleep. But he wondered how long will those habits continue before they stopped? And if they stopped, then what would that mean? Would it mean that he was over Rachel? Or would it mean that his heart stopped beating for her? Those thoughts were quickly erased from his mind as he knew

Rachel will forever hold a special place in his heart. Realizing he was having a sad moment, he immediately changed his thoughts to get him out of that down mood. Danny always did his best to avoid pity-parties, and was very conscious, at all times, to avoid stress and depression. He always kept his spirits up. That's what helped him get through all the time he spent by Rachel's side as she went through her last days.

Later that night, unable to sleep, He thought about what his son Chris said to him after they finished playing Texas Hold 'em poker. He was very tired of being alone, and made a firm decision that night that he was going to do his best to have companionship again. He knew that before today, he was only giving a half-hearted attempt, but now he was more determined than ever. He had to brush away feelings of guilt as if he was cheating on Rachel. Then he remembered what his daughter Vicky told him and that alleviated his guilt. She told him she didn't like to see him alone, and how her mom would want him to go on with his life. And moving on with this life to find another friend and soul-mate does not mean he is replacing Rachel, and how sad Rachel would be, watching him from Heaven pining his life away all alone. He now felt the time was right to seriously start life over again with another partner. He let out a groan as he dreaded the uncomfortable thought of searching and dating. This was something that was still very new to him since Rachel was the only woman he ever dated up until two years ago. He thought, 'I'm forty seven years old and I don't know how long it's going to take to find someone new who shares a lot of things in common with me. Things are so different in today's world. And based on the few dates I've had, I have no damn clue what the hell I'm doing. But, if I don't start now, then I might be eighty before I know it, and regretting being alone for all those years.'

*Looking up he said with sincerity, "Rachel? If you can hear me, then I want you to know that you'll always be in my heart, and I'll never stop loving you. Being alone really stinks, and I'm ready to work hard to find a new friend and companion again for as long as I live. I'm not looking to replace you. That will **never** happen. But I still feel like I'm not being loyal to you. Give me a sign that it's OK with you that I start looking." Within a few seconds a flash of lightning and the loud sound of nearby thunder startled Danny. "Crack! Boom! Crack!" Danny now laughing looked up and said, "Holy crap! A simple 'OK honey' would have sufficed. Jeez! I got your answer!" Leaning back and still quietly chuckling, he laid in bed with his hands behind his head staring into the darkness until sleep finally came to him.*

Danny Canton and his family live in Charlotte, North Carolina. He is a forty-seven year old, six foot tall, dark haired, handsome bank vice president, who works for a prominent nationwide banking institution. In addition to his great looks, he is in excellent physical condition as he works out at an exclusive fitness club three to four days a week religiously. Even while he's out of town on business trips, his company provides their executives with passes to the local fitness centers. Danny's personality is that of an extrovert, and was always fun to be around. He is very intelligent, diplomatic, and always very respectful regarding other people's situations. Since he became an eligible bachelor, he's being closely eyed by many females at work, and turns womens' heads wherever he goes. Over the years, he had many women interested in him, and some made passes at him while he was married. But he never crossed the line over to infidelity. He is a faithful and committed one-woman-man, and up until the day she passed away, Rachel was the only one for him. She was beautiful, and stood five foot ten inches tall, with long auburn hair and a gorgeous figure to match. She was a beautiful woman in every way imaginable, and turned his head even after twenty seven years of marriage. They made a handsome couple, and were always the envy of other people.

The only thing about Rachel's passing that he accepted well was that it was relatively quick. She suffered a stroke one night, at home after supper. Danny immediately carried her out to the car, and placed her into the back seat. While driving, he called his son and daughter to inform them, and had them contact the hospital Emergency Room that he was on his way. Vicky called the hospital to ensure the emergency team was prepared to receive and treat Rachel immediately. Danny made it to the emergency room in less than twenty minutes. Chris and Vicky were there waiting with the ER team. Rachel was responsive but in critical condition. After treating her and putting her in a hospital room hooked up to all the monitors she lived for five days before a blood clot formed, and made its way into her brain. During those five days he and his children spent as much time as possible with Rachel. Even though it was unexpected Danny was glad they had that time with her. He always looked at the positive side but, as anyone would expect, he took this very hard at first.

He and Rachel were empty nesters for a few years and they developed the routines that came with just the two of them. They were doing things they dreamed about for years that they could not do while raising their children. They made a great deal of plans such as cruising the Mediterranean, visiting Europe, Asia, and South America. Unfortunately, all those plans died along with Rachel. Danny and his children were resilient though. They relied on each other for support to get through the difficult stages of losing Rachel. With her passing so young, he did not want to bury her in the traditional funeral style that he and Rachel talked about when they believed they were going to live well into their eighties. Instead he had her cremated, and kept the urn containing Rachel's ashes on the mantle over the fireplace in the living room under their wedding portrait. Danny promised his kids he would someday bury Rachel's urn when he was ready to do so, and they respected his wishes. After about six months he gave away Rachel's clothes and had Chris and Vicky come over to go through and take whatever they wanted from Rachel's jewelry box.

He and Rachel raised two beautiful, intelligent, and well mannered children who went on to graduate college, marry, and start their own families. Both his children, now twenty eight year old adults, are professionals in their own fields. Chris, the oldest by sixty-six seconds, works as an Electrical Engineer for a local engineering firm. He is married to Donna Wilson, an Architect with a South Carolina company, whom he met while attending the University of Florida. Donna and her family are from the nearby town of Gastonia, North Carolina which is the neighboring city just south of Charlotte. It is also very convenient to have both families residing within a very short drive. Chris and Donna have one child, and plan on expanding their family by at least two more over the next five years. Vicky is a Registered Nurse, and holds the position of Assistant Director of Nursing at one of Charlotte's hospitals. She is married to

Stephen Fenton, a lawyer with a local law firm specializing in Real Estate law. She and Stephen also have one child but don't plan on having any more in the foreseeable future. Both of Danny's grown children are not only successful, but very independent.

Many times Danny thought of how fortunate he was that his wife was around to help raise their children through adulthood. If it wasn't for Rachel, he could have easily had a very difficult time as a single parent. Rachel was always there to help the kids with all kinds of things that he did not feel comfortable or knowledgeable enough to handle, especially with his daughter. Now his kids are grown, and his relationship went from father and disciplinarian, to father and great friend. Being a friend to his kids is something Danny is very good at doing. He's also very proud of them, and boasts about being a 'young' grandfather, though he doesn't look like the stereotypical 'grandfather' at all. With his youthful appearance, his age could pass for late thirties.

Friday or Saturday nights were reserved for friends or family get-togethers at Danny's house. This was something of a tradition that at least twice a month Danny and Rachel hosted some kind of gathering. It was either dinner, or just cocktails, or what he really enjoyed, which was a game of Texas Hold 'em poker with friends and or family. Not only did he love to play, he was excellent at the game. He was good enough to enter and *win some of the amateur tournaments at the casinos in North Carolina, and during his trips with Rachel to the casinos in Mississippi, and New Jersey. Rachel's lessons worked so well on Danny that he took his game to a higher level, and mastered it. She went from beating him when they played together, to watching him develop an expertise in the art and science of the game. She saw him win hands and matches with only an intimidating expression on his face, while bluffing his opponents with absolutely nothing for a hand. He loved his work and his family, and despite his friends trying to encourage him to play poker professionally, he decided professional poker was 'not in the cards' for him. He was very satisfied with where he was in his life with his; job, friends, and family. Now he was about to embark on his search for a new love in his life. But before he did that, he made sure he had his Last Will and Testament written to include only his children and grandchildren. Being financially well off he did not want to have any issues with anyone who was looking to use him for their financial freedom. He wanted to be sure that, if and when he found his new soul mate, she was going to accept him for who he is, and not for what he has.*

Chapter 2
A New Twist To Dating

Danny *spent a great deal of time in deep conversation with his close friends regarding the seriousness of his commitment to search for a new soulmate. Most of the time the topic of the discussion surrounded the issue of the methods by which people meet and agree to date in the current times. His long-time married friends were not able to give him much direction, but his newly divorced friends made him very nervous. They told him that finding a date in 2017 was* nothing *like it was when they were in their late teens and early twenties during the period between the late 1980's and early 1990's. When he was told that the majority of dating was now done by arranging a date using online website applications, he was mortified. He told his friends that he remembered the exact opposite with internet meetings, and how people who met on the internet in the 1990's were putting themselves in a very dangerous position. He thought, 'My how times have dramatically changed. What* *used to put people at serious risk was now the preferred way of meeting!"*

With the help of his son Chris, and his daughter Vicky, Danny registered with several internet dating sites. He also took this opportunity to use this as quality time spent with his children. He valued, and trusted their opinions on how to set up his accounts, and all the other intricate details that went along with the information for narrowing down his online searches. His kids warned him though, to always question the people he chatted with, because there were plenty of 'posers' *on these sites.* Posers *are people who are not truthful, and post things about themselves that are outright lies. Things such as pictures, accomplishments, their likes and dislikes, their professions, careers, and sometimes even their sexual identity. This did not sit well with him. He said to his kids, "You know me. I value integrity and I'm probably going to wind up cursing someone out if I find out they lied to me. If I meet them in public, I'll most likely leave them and walk away."*

Both his kids requested that he just be cool and diplomatic in handling the situation. Chris said, "Dad, you're from a different era and used to old school *ways. I could see you walking away from someone you found to be a phony right in the middle of dessert in a restaurant and leaving them with the bill!" Danny answered, "Why not? I don't do well with liars or phony people. Oh I'd pay for my meal and leave a tip. But I hope that walking out on them will teach them a lesson they should have seen coming. I couldn't give a damn about what they might think of me. Guys? I've got a feeling this is going to be a real eye opener for me. But I have a question for both of you. How do you two know so much about the ins and outs of these dating sites? I mean, both of you did not do much dating, and you've been married for years now."*

Vicky laughed as she answered, "We've got single friends our age who are on these sites and they tell us all kinds of wild stories. I sat by my friends' computers or smart-phones and watched them interact with people on these sites. I even helped them with setting up their accounts and coached them on what to write about themselves to help them attract the kind of person they're looking for. But I always encouraged them to be completely honest." Chris nodded, chuckled, and said, "Yeah, my buddies from work told me all kinds of crazy crap that happened to them with dates from these online dating services. Most are really good dates, but the interesting conversations are mostly about the whack-jobs they meet! Those are hysterical!"

Danny shook his head and said, "After hearing all this, I'm thinking that being single and alone is looking pretty damn good after all!" Vicky looked at him and said, "C'mon dad. Just give it a chance. What do you have to lose?" Danny shrugged his shoulders and sarcastically answered, "My sanity! My career! My standing in the community! My life! You name it! Seems to me like the old school ways *of meeting someone in...let's say, the grocery store, or the department store, and getting their phone number and arranging a date is...out of style." Chris responded, "That's right dad. Doing things like that, in this day and age, will get you labeled as a 'creeper', or a 'stalker', and you might even get the cops called on you for harassment." Danny exclaimed, "What!? Are you kidding me!? Simple harmless conversation before asking for a date in a public place can have those kinds of consequences? Holy shit! What the hell am I getting myself into?" Chris and Vicky laughed hysterically at their father's outburst and the distorted expression of disgust on his face. Trying to comfort him Vicky said, "Hey dad! You're worrying wayyyy too much, and blowing this wayyyy out of proportion. Just be cool and we'll help you. When anyone contacts you,* let us *help you screen them." Shaking his head and smiling Danny replied, "Ok. But you better be prepared to accompany me as my chaperone, 'cause I believe I'm wayyyy over my head in these waters. From what you've told me, I don't know if I could trust anyone on these sites! But...I'll give it a try. Man oh man! I must be nuts to do this! Ok. Ok. I promise I'll be cool."*

Turning her attention to the sound coming from the computer, a symbol on the screen caught Vicky's eye.

Excited by what she saw she said, "Hey look dad! You just got a message from someone! Go ahead and open it, and let's see who it's from." The picture next to the symbol was that of a beautiful fair skinned, red haired woman, with ruby red lipstick. Danny said slowly, "Oooh! That looks interesting. Maybe I rushed to judgment here guys. Let's see what she wrote." Clicking on the symbol, all eyes were on the screen anxiously awaiting the message. As they read it, Danny's jaw dropped in horror to the request. Under his breath, but audible for the others to hear he whispered, "Awe...Holy crap! What the...!" Chris and Vicky were snorting as they tried very hard not to erupt out loud in laughter. It read: 'Hello sexy man. My name is Lucy and have I got some plans for you! Are you into whips and chains? I am. How about messaging me back and tell me when we can get together for some very unique fun? If you know what I mean! I'm waiting for you!'

Danny's fascination and excitement turned to disgust, and his face turned red, as he was embarrassed from the message since his kids were there reading it too. Calming down for a moment between bouts of hysterical laughter, Vicky put her hand on her forehead and said, "Oh my God!" Chris burst out in laughter and said, "Holy crap dad! I never expected a person like that coming from this top rated dating site! Did that picture

Vicky posted of you look like you're into S&M painful pleasure? Hahaha!"

Incensed by the messaged Danny placed his hands over the keyboard and typed the following reply: 'Dear Madam S&M, I would have to be blind drunk, strung out on crack, inoculated against every disease known to mankind including rabies and committed to a mental ward before even thinking about being on the opposite side of the same state with you! Quickly do the world a favor and seek professional help in the form of a psychiatrist and be sure he prescribes lots of red and blue pills. PS - When you see the shrink, leave the damn whips and chains at home. Or better yet...recycle them. In other words, No Thanks Lucy-fer!' Clicking send and stepping back he asked, "You think that was clear enough for this sicko-psycho to understand? My first message just had to be from 'Lucy-the-Lunatic'! That's as cool as I can be with someone like her."

Vicky blushed as she continued to laugh out loud, but was too embarrassed to respond. Chris opened up and said, "Don't worry dad. You know there are all kinds of people out there!" Danny laughed as he replied, "Oh yeah? But this one does not fit in any of those categories. Wow! I don't want either of you mentioning this to anyone. Understand? I don't need to hear remarks from others about this or any other crazy-ass messages I may receive in the future. Let's just forget about the freaks and *focus on the 'decent' ones...*IF there are any out there! Ok?*" Vicky and Chris snickered as they shook their heads in agreement. Danny continued, "Oh and by the way Vicky, change that picture of me you posted on this site. I don't want to attract anyone else like that* Lucy *character again." Vicky still snickering said, "Ok dad. I'll post the one with you in your bathing suit taken when you and mom were on Grand Cayman Island's '7 Mile Beach'." Shaking his finger at her he responded, "*Don't you dare! I'll probably get responses from all the weird women* posing *as mermaids and asking me for a date at the bottom of the Atlantic with their father Neptune!"*

After posting a handsome picture of Danny in his tuxedo from a recent black tie affair Vicky logged off the website and shut down the computer. The three of them sat down for a soft drink, talked, and enjoyed a few laughs for a while before finishing their visit and leaving. When his kids pulled out of his driveway and headed for their respective home, Danny shut and locked the front door, turned off the lights, and headed off to bed. Before bedding down for the night he laid in bed and amused himself with thoughts of who he was going to encounter from these websites. Little did he know he was in for some wild rides ahead, courtesy of the internet dating sites.

Chapter 3
Peggy

Checking *messages from his dating site the night after Vicky set it up, Danny came across and interesting one. It read:*

Hi there! My name is Peggy and I'm interested in chatting with you. If you're interested, please tag me with your message on a date and time. You're really handsome and I like how well you organized your site.
Looking forward to following up with you,
Peggy

As he looked over Peggy's neatly decorated website and tasteful pictures of her, he thought, 'Well that's a lot better, and more of what I expect from a pleasant looking person in my age bracket. Pretty woman who appears to be on the conservative side of the line. Ok. Let me send her a message.' He replied to her message with the following: 'Hello Peggy. Thank you for contacting me and for your compliments. I would certainly like to chat with you as well. How about tomorrow night at 9pm? Danny.' Hitting the send button he waited for the site to confirm his message was sent. After receiving the confirmation, he decided to turn off his computer and watch the evening news before going to bed.

Catching himself before shutting down the computer, the website alerted him with a short telephone-like ring, signaling that he received another message. Curiously, he stopped to check it out. It was a reply from Peggy. With a look of surprise on his face he muttered, "Wow. That was quick! Let's see what she has to say." Opening the message it read, 'Tomorrow night at 9p works great for me! Chat with you then! Have a wonderful nigh Danny. Peg!'

Danny snickered as he closed the website and shutdown his computer. He stood up from his desk, stretched and yawned for a moment, then turned off the light and walked out of his office and headed for his bedroom. After brushing his teeth and washing his face he dried himself off. Then he laid down on his bed and turned on the television. Watching the news, but distracted in deep thought, he was a little nervous about the 'chat' he was going to have with Peggy. Picking up his cell phone he called his daughter, and asked her to pull up his dating site, and requested she check out Peggy, as he wanted to get her opinion. Vicky agreed and told him she would call him the next day with her thoughts. After hanging up the phone, Danny turned off the TV and the light, and within a few minutes he was sound asleep.

Rising and yawning after he was awakened by his alarm clock, Danny sat up in his bed. He smiled with his eyes closed as he enjoyed the aroma from the coffee maker as the smell of fresh brewed coffee made its way up to his bedroom. Stretching his arms he muttered, "Gosh that smells so good." After a restless sleep from some anxiety about his upcoming chat with Peggy he really needed that caffeine. Putting on his slippers, he then rubbed his eyes before walking downstairs to the kitchen for that first cup of Brazilian Dark Roast Java he enjoyed so much.

After taking his second sip his cell phone rang. It was his daughter. Muttering before answering he said, "She never calls this early unless something's up." Answering the phone he said, "Hey honey. Everything OK?" Vicky answered, "Hey dad. Yeah, everything's fine here. I don't usually bother you this early, but I wanted to tell you something." Relieved there was no emergency he replied, "Ok Vic. What is it?" With a little snicker Vicky said, "You asked me to check your website to follow up on that person who wants to chat with you tonight. Well, I did. By her very tidy webpage, this Peggy initially looks pretty persnickety but somewhat charming. I looked at the background info she posted. Everything looked pretty good and initially seemed down to earth and normal to your standards. Then a funny thing happened." Danny smiled and said, "Oh boy. What happened?"

Vicky continued to snicker as she said, "Well dad, on this website, if you 'tag' a person, like you both did to each other, then your site notifies you when the people you 'tagged' are actively online. That allows you to send them an instant message that you will immediately see in your message log on your screen." Danny said, "Ok. I understand. So what happened already?" Vicky answered, "Dad. Within about two minutes Peggy sent you five messages. Nothing outrageous or silly. Just messages asking things like; How's it going?; Are you free to talk?; Why aren't you answering me?; Etcetera."

Danny didn't see anything wrong with this and responded, "Well Vic. Maybe she's lonely and a little anxious. I don't want to read too much into that. So what do you think?" She replied, "Maybe you're right dad. I got the first impression that she's a little desperate and perhaps...a little obsessive too. But then, maybe I'm being a concerned and overprotective daughter. I thought it was a little odd because that's not something that I would do, and it's not something I've ever seen any of my friends do either." Danny chuckled and said, "That's OK honey. I'm glad you're looking out for me. For a moment you had me worried. I'm a big boy, and while I appreciate *your honest and open feedback, I guess I'll have to see for myself. It's getting late and I've got to jump in the shower and don't have much time. Anything else unusual before I let you go?" She answered, "No. That's about it. Just seemed a little strange to me. Not psycho-ax-murderer strange. But...just strange. OK dad. Call me after you chat with Peggy. Love ya. Bye!" Danny said, "Over Have a great day sweetheart." After hanging up the phone, He went about his daily routine of showering, shaving, and leaving for work. He met with his work friends for a short breakfast in the office building's restaurant located on the ground floor before going to his office. He enjoyed an uneventful day's work and then it was back home for the evening.*

It was ten minutes until nine when he logged into his account on the dating site. He smiled as he noticed he had over one hundred twenty comments, or hits as the website referred to them. These 'hits' were very short comments and meant to usually give the person receiving them a compliment. He laughed at some of the one liners as he read them out loud. Talking out loud he said, "Did not expect so many hits. From lots of pretty girls and...hahaha...some guys too. Oh crap. That's too funny." Just as he was reading through his hits he was notified that it was nine o'clock and time for his 'chat' as Peggy messaged him to click on the website's chat button. Glad that she knew how to navigate the site, he clicked on the symbol which took him to a private 'chat room' where Peggy anxiously awaited. They typed their conversation via instant message to each other as follows:

Peggy: *Hey Danny! So glad you made it. How are you doing tonight?*

Danny: *I'm doing great. How about yourself?*

Peggy: *I'm just peachy! Well, where do we start?*

Danny: *I'm really new at this. Never been on a dating site before so I'll start by telling you something about me. I'm a forty-seven year old widower and the father of two grown children. A son and a daughter who are both married and on their own. My kids wasted no time making me a grandfather as I have two grandchildren. I am thoroughly enjoying my grandkids. How about you?*

Peggy: *That's wonderful. Well as for me, I'm forty-nine years old. Single. Never been married. But I did come close a couple of times. I live with my parents since I don't like living alone. I teach elementary school. Third graders. I taught high school for a couple of years but I like teaching little children better so I stayed at the elementary school level. Not marrying and not having children is why I like the elementary level. Those are my kids. At least for a while during the day. I get to give them* *back. And some of them I am only too glad to give back at the end of the day. What kind of work do you do?*

Danny: *That's funny. Well for better or for worse my kids are permanent. Thank goodness they turned out fine. I'm very proud of them. As for my profession I'm a bank VP. Many years ago I graduated from the University of North Carolina where I majored in Banking and Finance. I've been in banking here in Charlotte ever since. I really enjoy the work. It's very rewarding and gave me what I needed to build my life. Ok Peggy how about telling me about your personality and your hobbies?*

Peggy: *That's great about your children and very interesting about your profession. Banking and high finance have always been way over my head. I'm not good in those areas. My dad helps me when it comes time to those matters. About my personality. I am really good over the phone or the internet when communicating with people. But in person I'm pretty shy and reserved. As for hobbies, I love to read, take quiet walks in the park and outdoors, and I like old movies, especially suspense ones in black and white. How about you? Your personality and hobbies?*

Danny: *I'm an extrovert. I love to be around my family and friends. I'm also very comfortable around large audiences and crowds of people whether I know them or not. I speak before Boards of Directors, Finance*

Committees, and at formal and informal banking functions. I get to know people very quickly so I guess you can say people are not strangers to me for very long. As for hobbies, besides spending a lot of time with my children and grandchildren, I like to stay in as great condition as possible so I exercise anywhere from 4 to 5 days a week. Another hobby I have that I take tremendous pleasure in is playing poker. I like to watch movies once in a while and my taste runs to adventure and suspense. I like a good plot. Today's movies don't interest me much. I like the older gangster movies. Well Peggy. You seem pretty down to earth. Since I'm brand new to this site I am not sure of what to do from this point. Would it be too soon if I asked you if you would like to join me for dinner? Say Friday night at 7pm as my guest at Lucray's Restaurant? I'm not a very good internet chat person. I prefer in-person meeting and conversation.

Peggy*: I think it would be nice to meet you in person. Getting to know someone is always better in person than chatting over the internet. Friday at 7pm. I heard that's a very nice restaurant. I hope you understand I'm a little nervous.*

Danny*: I completely understand. This place has a nice quiet atmosphere and it's always very pleasant and safe. They only take reservations so they have a lot of information about their patrons. So is that a yes?*

Peggy: *Yes. That sounds wonderful. I will start to get ready from now.*

Danny: *(chuckling as he's typing) Don't be nervous Peggy. You have plenty of time to get ready. That's a few days from now. See you then.*

Peggy: *Oh yes. How silly of me. I'm fine. See you then.*

Peggy exited the chat room almost immediately. Danny was still smiling as he thought about Peggy's comment that she was 'getting ready' for a date that was not going to take place for several days. He chalked that comment up to her being nervous about their date and did not give it much further thought at all.

Shutting down his computer he left his office and went to his bedroom. He laid on his bed and tried to watch TV before going to sleep but was a bit restless. Turning off the TV set he reached for his cell phone from the night stand adjacent to his bed. Pressing a speed dial button he called his daughter. Answering the phone on the third ring they conversed for about ten minutes. He explained to Vicky that the chat with Peggy went well, and he did not notice any quirks or issues, other than she seemed nervous and anxious and that was what he expected. He also told her he set up a date on Friday for dinner, and if that went well, he planned to go to an exclusive club later for drinks and dancing. There were no concerns voiced between Danny and Vicky and everything sounded like a pretty low key for an old-fashioned night out on the town. She was happy for her father, and of course, she requested that he gave her a full report on how his date turned out.

After his conversation with Vicky, he decided to use his cell phone to check his company e-mail account. Danny read through a few e-mails he received after he came home from work. Nothing urgent. Before putting his phone back on the nightstand he noticed an icon on the screen. It was a Texas Hold 'em poker game application (app) he downloaded over a month ago. He hadn't had time to play and forgot all about it up until then. Still bored and restless he decided to open the app and play to see what this internet game involved. Before any play, he went through the initial set up. Not wanting to use his actual identity he made up a name and used an avatar provided by the game instead of his actual picture.

He chose the name Clint and an avatar of a cowboy for his picture so he could play anonymously. The game provided every new player with an initial stack of free chips. Players could purchase additional chips if they ran out or delete the game off their cell phone if they didn't like it.

He found the game interesting and challenging and he continued playing...and winning. The biggest challenge was playing against others from the privacy of your phone where you could not see other players' faces. Instead of reading faces, now he had to determine his opponents' positions by their betting habits. Most were completely reckless in their play while some were actually pretty good. The game allowed members to type comments and displayed them to all at the bottom of the screen. A few people were rude but mostly comical and witty. Each table allowed a maximum of seven players. Those who left the game were almost immediately replaced by others. Danny was enjoying the game and even posted some comments of his own. The game also allowed players to 'tag' other players as a 'friend' so you could follow them or join them later in another game. He was having fun engaging others in conversation through their comments and he was winning most of the games he played.

A little while later a female player joined the game due to a vacancy courtesy of Danny's winning hand. Her avatar was a cowgirl and her name was 'Pretty Cowgirl'. Danny smiled and typed his welcoming comment, 'Howdy Partner!' She commented back, 'Yahoo Buckaroo! Howdy Clint!'

Danny smiled and continued to play. Of all the people at the table Pretty Cowgirl and Danny were the best players. He thought to himself, 'This Pretty Cowgirl is a pretty damn good player.' She even beat him several times as he did her. Gauging her play by her betting habits and style was tough. They threw witty comments back and forth. He tagged her as a 'friend' before glancing at the clock on his night stand.

"Oh crap! It's after four already! I'd better stop here and catch a few hours sleep. Thank goodness I don't have a busy schedule today!" he said out loud. Before leaving the table and turning off the game, he sent a message to 'Pretty Cowgirl' thanking her for her excellent play, and looking forward to another match. She commented back on how much she enjoyed his challenging play and that she was always ready for a rematch. His final comment was, 'Anytime Partner!' before exiting and closing the game. Returning the phone to its charger on the night stand, he turned out the light, and within a few minutes he was sound asleep.

A couple of hours later his alarm sounded. His eyes opened slowly as he stretched out his arms and groaned out loud saying, "I'm gonna pay for this today. But it was worth it." Getting up and out of bed quickly he walked to the bathroom where he brushed his teeth before getting into the shower. The rest of the morning was routine. The coffee was brewed and ready for him after he dressed and came down to the kitchen. Pouring himself a large cup of coffee in his travel mug he looked around as he took a few sips. Turning off the coffee maker he checked all the appliances in the kitchen before setting the house alarm, then locked the door as he exited the house, and drove off to work. A pretty slow routine day was what he needed after a couple hours of sleep. After work, it was off to the gym for a short work out, then home for dinner and a good night's sleep. He did manage to get in a few hands of poker on his cell phone's gaming app, but he limited his play to half an hour. He was hooked on the game.

The rest of the week at work went by quickly. All routine matters and nothing out of the ordinary. It was now Friday and Danny was preparing for his date with Peggy. He made a reservation at Lucray's earlier that week. Arriving at the restaurant at 6:50 that evening the Maitre d' advised him that his table was ready and his party had been waiting since six o'clock. Danny thanked him and followed him to the table. On the way he laughed to himself at Peggy's arriving an hour early and chalked it up to her being nervous and wanting to make a good first impression. He then had a scary thought the he hoped she had not been drinking alcohol for almost an hour already! Taking a deep breath before stopping at the table, he braced himself for the introduction. The Maitre d' waited for him to get to the table before he nodded and left them alone.

Danny's and Peggy's eyes met and they both smiled. She was very pretty and dressed in an attractive pink dress. He broke the ice by extending a single red rose to her and introducing himself, "Hello Peggy. It's nice to meet you. You look very lovely." He shook her hand before taking his seat across from her. Peggy had a hard time keeping eye contact as she blushed from Danny's introduction.

She cleared her throat and nervously responded, "Hello Danny. It's nice to meet you too and thank you for the beautiful rose and compliment. Sorry I was here so early. I did not want to be delayed by traffic. I must have drank several glasses of water since I arrived." He smiled and was relieved it was water and not vodka. He said, "Glad you made it here alright. So are you ready to eat or would you like a cocktail?"

Avoiding as much eye contact as possible she responded with a nervous giggle, "Oh no. I don't drink very much. It usually goes straight to my head. My friends call me a lightweight." He dealt with all kinds of personalities and knowing how to handle Peggy's nervousness he said, "That's fine. We can skip that. Why don't we order dinner now and talk while we're waiting for our food. I just want to assure you there's nothing to be nervous about. Please relax and let's enjoy the time together. OK?"

She smiled and nodded as she looked around, and still blushing she said, "That's fine. That's me! I'm good over the phone and internet, but in person I'm very *shy." He tried to comfort her by answering, "I understand." They both looked through the menu and decided to order their food. They had a good conversation throughout dinner. He managed to help Peggy open up and come out of her shell now and then.*

During their conversation he noticed an elderly couple sitting a few tables away. While talking to Peggy he noticed the couple would sometimes stare at him and smile. Early on, Danny did not give it much thought, but after a while he was feeling a little uncomfortable with the constant grinning, smiling, and nodding that accompanied their stares. After Danny and Peggy finished their dinner they ordered dessert and coffee and conversed some more. The elderly couple continued to stare and smile but he tried to not pay them any attention, but he could no longer help himself.

He excused himself to go to the Men's room. On the way he stopped at the elderly couple's table. He said "Good evening. Please excuse me but I could not help notice that you kept staring at me since I've been here. Do you know me?" The man spoke up and said, "Oh I'm sorry if we made you nervous or upset. My wife and I were just admiring what a handsome young couple you both make. It reminds us of us when we were younger." Danny smiled and said, "Oh. That's fine. Thank you for the compliment and I hope you enjoy your evening," as he walked off.

Rejoining Peggy at the table he saw that she now seemed very nervous and fidgety. She had her left hand over her mouth and stared off to her right while nervously tapping the table with the fingers of her right hand. With concern in his voice he asked, "What's the matter Peggy? Is anything wrong?" Peggy looked at Danny, took her hand away from her mouth and answered, "Um...I don't know Danny. I mean...I think things are OK."

He was now confused as he waited for her to explain. Still nervously tapping she continued, "Well I mean...I want...um...I,,,I want to know where we're going?" Danny still giving her the benefit of the doubt, blaming her nervousness on the date, innocently answered, "Well if we hit it off at dinner I planned to take you to an exclusive night club for drinks and dancing, and for us to get to know more about each other. Is that OK?"

Even more nervous now Peggy shook her head and responded, "That's...not what I mean. I mean...Um...Since we've known each other for a while now I...Uh...I want to know where this relationship is going? You see those people seated at that table?" Peggy pointed to the elderly couple who were staring at them and who were now smiling and waving. She continued, "Those are my parents. They are very anxious to see me get married and want to know what the status of our relationship is and where we're going from this point."

Danny was dumbfounded with Peggy's answer and explanation! He could not believe what he was hearing. Believing it was a joke and wanting to laugh at first, he then realized by the look on Peggy's face, that she was serious. He did not want to hurt Peggy's feelings before giving some thought to his response. Thinking of the right thing to say, he tried to comfort Peggy by calmly saying, "Look Peggy. We have not established any kind of a relationship. We simply met, for the first time, to see how much we had in common. And IF this went well then move on. But move on slowly. Very slowly. What you're saying is pretty shocking and I'm not ready to make any kind of commitment like that. We hardly know anything about each other. As far as I see it, relationships take time to develop. Lots and lots of time."

Now beet-red faced, Peggy looked down at the table and said, "I really don't know. I mean I thought some people hit it off right away and I really felt like you were the one for me. Oh my...I'm so embarrassed." Feeling sorry for her he said, "Please don't feel embarrassed. You're a lovely woman and I believe you'll find what you're looking for. I'm not ready for anything like what you've said with anyone. Let's just call it a night and go our own ways. I don't want you to feel hurt. I believe that's best. How about you?"

She looked up at Danny, sighed and said, "I guess you're right. I keep doing this whenever I get a date. The only thing different about this date is that you didn't jump out of your skin, scream, and run like all the others. You were really nice about it." He asked, "Are you going to be OK?" Still not making eye contact and continuously blushing a deep red from embarrassment she answered, "Oh yes. I'll be fine. My parents will take me home." Danny said, "Good. I guess it's goodbye then Peggy. I hope you find happiness." Then he stood up and shook her hand before meeting up with the Maitre d' to pay the bill and leave. Danny avoided Peggy's parents and could not get out of the restaurant fast enough!

Getting into his car and driving off, he waited until he was close to home before calling his daughter. Answering the phone on the first ring Vicky immediately said, "Hey dad. I didn't expect your call until tomorrow. Let me guess? Things did not go well on your date with Peggy! Are you OK?"

Danny's chuckle was part laughter and part frustration as he answered, "Holy Jeez! What an experience! I never saw that one coming! But let me first say that your assessment was spot on. Man oh man is this one up for a story in that 'Believe It Or Not' book. I'm glad I got out of the restaurant with my life intact." Almost in a panic Vicky asked, "Life intact! Dad, are you alright?! What happened? Where are you?" Laughing he answered, *"I'm fine and on my way home. Relax. No one is hurt. Physically I mean. Let me tell you about it."*

*After explaining all the details of his date he could hear Vicky laughing hysterically. When she calmed down long enough to regain her self-control she responded, "Are you kidding me? She actually brought her parents there? And expected a marriage proposal out of you after dinner? Oh my God! That's twisted and that's a scream!" Danny replied, "How the hell did you think I felt when she asked me: Where are we going from here? I told her I planned to take her dancing at the club. I didn't know she wanted to go dancing down the aisle? Holy shit! And all the time with her creepy parents watching, staring, and waving at me. They're all bat-shit crazy. What's ironic is that I told her I was taking her to a place where she should feel safe. Little did I realize it was a place for my safety, not hers." Vicky continued to laugh as she said, "Dad. That tops **all** I've heard about a screwy date. Even my friends never encountered something like that! Wait until Chris hears this! He's going to..."*

Interrupting her he pleaded, "Don't talk to Chris or anyone! Please? Let me talk to him. It was humiliating enough watching the Maitre d' and the wait staff holding in their laughter as well as the other patrons trying to keep from howling. Peggy's voice carried pretty good and I saw the other people there almost falling out of their chairs trying to catch every word of the conversation there at the end. For a minute at that point I was waiting for someone to come out of hiding holding a video camera like they did in those 'Hidden Camera' shows where they pull pranks on unsuspecting people. But it never happened. I hope no one was filming this because I don't want this scene blasted all over the internet. I surely won't show my face around there for a while. But I kept my cool...and let her down easy. I'm going home now and I'm going to pour myself a strong scotch on the rocks, and I'm NOT turning on my computer."

*Vicky felt bad for her father but still managing to get in a last jab said, "Ok dad. You do that. Just remember...I love you....And so does Peggy! Hahahahaha! Sorry. I couldn't help that one. You'll be fine. It's frustrating but don't let that stop your search. People like mom are one in a million. You'll find someone. Just don't give up. OK?" Laughing back he said, "Yeah you're right. Looking at the bright side...Well at least Peggy loves me too and she was trying to solve my problem of finding a soul mate immediately. Hahaha! Gotta laugh about it honey. But I need you to remember I'm not trying to replace mom. She's irreplaceable! I'm trying to find a companion to go through life together. But if all my dates are like tonight's date then, **alone IS,** an option! Ok honey. I'll let you go. Kiss the baby for me. I'll see you soon. Love you. Good night!" She replied, "Take care dad. Love you too. Bye!"*

Hanging up the phone Danny arrived home. After entering his house he loosened his tie and poured a strong serving of scotch in a goblet. Then he sat down in the living room looking at the wedding picture of him and Rachel as he sipped his drink. He sat there thinking of how he could not believe the events of this date. Shaking his head and laughing as he relived the last scene at the restaurant with Peggy, he looked at Rachel's picture and said, "If I didn't know better I could swear you were pulling one of your pranks on me. I could picture you up in Heaven tonight, gathered with your angel-buddies watching me, and laughing your wings off!"

After finishing his drink, he walked to the kitchen and placed his glass into the dishwasher. He turned off all the lights then went upstairs to his bedroom where he changed his clothes and washed up before turning in for the night. Unable to sleep he decided to play the poker game on his cell phone. Tapping the game icon on his phone's screen opened the game. He proceeded to the screen that showed him all the available games. Before selecting a game he received an invitation to play by a tagged friend. It was Pretty Cowgirl. He smiled as he clicked on the invitation and within a few seconds he joined the table with her and several other players.

They conversed back and forth by exchanging instant messages that everyone at the table could also *read. After a while of focusing on the game he forgot about his date with Peggy. He enjoyed the witty exchange with Pretty Cowgirl as they played for several hours. Both of them were the big winners at the table and soon they faced each other. With no one else playing at their table, their conversation grew deeper as they played cautiously to conserve their chip positions. Without giving away either one's true identity or where they lived, they relaxed and thoroughly enjoyed the topics they discussed. They realized they had quite a bit in common.*

Not wanting to lose all their chips, after a few hands of fairly even play, they decided to call it a night since it was getting late. They decided to end the game, and signed off in corny Texas style, with messages such as, 'Gotta hit the dusty trail,' and 'So long Buckaroo.' Danny's last messaged was, 'See ya at the next showdown partner', before shutting down the game. Tonight though, after the game, they both stayed up and fantasized about what each one thought the other one was like. Their fantasies included looks, personality, sexiness, and what it would be like to be together. He wanted and needed those thoughts just as much as Pretty Cowgirl did.

Chapter 4
Pretty Cowgirl

Pretty *Cowgirl sat in bed after closing the game on her phone and thought about Clint, which made her smile. She thought, 'I wonder what this guy is like. He sure seems smart, easy going, and funny. It's nice to have an enjoyable conversation with a guy without all the facades and sexual innuendos. But then, it's a text conversation from the safety of a cell phone. Well I'll just keep playing and talking. I need that after my last catastrophic relationship. I need to know that there are decent guys out there...even if I don't know who they are, or what they look like. It's late, and at least I can get to sleep with a smile on my face, and leave all of this up to my imagination.' Turning out her bedroom light she turned over on her side and went to sleep. Her last thoughts were of Clint, and when they would meet again at the next game and talk. She dreamt that she met 'Clint' and he turned out to be a handsome, intelligent, caring, and considerate man. The scenes were great and he was all she fantasized about in a man. When she awakened* *early the next morning she wanted to go back to sleep and continue dreaming but was unable to do so. Finally she fell back asleep but this time it was a deep dreamless sleep.*

Her name is Christy Darren. She and her only daughter Stacie live in Orlando, Florida. She's a forty five year old, blonde haired, hazel-eyed, beautiful woman with medium tanned skin. Standing five foot eight she is in excellent physical condition with a slender sexy figure. Christy was widowed eight years ago when she lost her husband John in a single car wreck. She, like Danny, had a great marriage that tragically ended too soon. She and John were very close and involved in all areas of their everyday lives. They loved and played all kinds of sports. Sometimes they played together on the same team, whether it was mixed softball, bowling, or it was just the two of them going on fishing trips to nearby lakes, or deep sea fishing in the Atlantic or the Gulf.

Christy graduated from the University of Florida with a degree in Marketing and is a diehard Florida Gator fan. Using that degree she took a job with a major Pharmaceutical company and worked her way up to a Regional Directorship position. Along with her husband's life insurance proceeds, her job paid her well enough to manage her home, lifestyle, and her twenty four year old daughter's education. After her husband's passing she focused her life on raising Stacie and becoming best friends with her.

Stacie Darren attended and graduated from the University of Central Florida in Orlando so she could commute from home and stay close to her mom. She didn't want her mom to be alone and didn't want to burden her with the additional costs of going away to college. It was good for both of them. But since her graduation, Stacie's interests and social life were going in other directions which took time away from her mom. She earned her degree in Nursing and worked as a Registered Nurse with a large Orlando hospital. She made a lot of friends and with her nursing job she was now spending a considerable amount of time with others. While Christy had friends from work she had only a few trusted friends that she spent time with to fill the void left when Stacie's life drastically changed due to her new commitments.

Being the beauty she is Christy attracted many men. Unfortunately all of them wanted her for her looks and figure but none of them were looking for a long term relationship. Bluntly put, it was sex they were after, and with her beauty and sexy figure, that's the first thing that attracted everyone to her. But Christy was smarter than that and knew the game well. All too often she agreed to a date only to end up driving home early after dinner and drinks were over. Many dates ended early because the guy was either, frustrated when she did not accept his invitation to go back to his apartment, or he was just plain boring. She was nobody's fool and she was committed, come hell or high water, to her plan of taking her time to let a relationship develop first before anything physical took place. Some dates worried her as some of the guys became angry because she refused their outright demand, or pushed away their physical advances, for sex.

Christy was not an easy target. Early into her marriage she and her husband took self defense classes in martial arts and they practiced often to maintain their skill level. With her training and high self-esteem she walked confidently and was well aware of her surroundings and situations. She advanced her skill level as she and her daughter attended a school in martial arts together for twelve years. Both she and Stacie earned second degree Black Belts in Taekwondo and both won gold medals in full contact competition in state tournaments in several years.

Saturday morning was a day to sleep in and rest from a long work week of report preparations, traveling, and long meetings. A knock on her bedroom door woke her up. It was her daughter checking in with her. Opening the door Stacie poked her head in and softly said, "You awake mom?" Christy softly whispered back, "No. I'm still asleep." Turning over and snickering as she rubbed her eyes she continued, "Of course I'm awake now

that you knocked and called out to me. What time is it?"
Stacie answered, "In a little while it's gonna be Tuesday.
Hahaha! Mom, it's already after eleven. I thought you
had a date last night. What happened?"

Now sitting up in bed, Christy shook her head as
her fingers combed back her hair, and with a look of
disgust answered, "I called Gary at his home an hour
before we were going to meet and found out something
awful about him." Stacie said, "Oh no mom. What was
that? Is he gay or something?" Christy laughed and said,
"Oh no. I could deal with that. This was a horrible
shocking surprise! The person who answered the phone
was Gary's wife! That dirty rotten dog is married! What a
jerk! It was awkward for me and I apologized to the poor
thing. I told her I never knew that her husband was a two-
timing son-of-a-bitch. After I hung up the phone with her
I decided not to call his cell phone."

Stacie, now standing there stunned and feeling
bad for her mom asked, "What did you do after that?"
Christy laughed and answered, "I went to the gym for a
short workout. Punched and kicked the bag to get my
frustrations out, took a shower, and went out for dinner
with my friend Susan. While we were having dinner he
texted me and inquired as to: why I was late. I guess he
did not go home after his golf game to get an update on
the news that he's a married man from his wife. Anyway I
texted him back. I instructed him to go home and explain

to his wife why he was not having dinner with her *tonight. He never texted or called me after that. My guess is he either left on the first flight out of the country or he went home to face his wife who,* I hoped, *gave him a good ass-kicking out of the house! What a turd he turned out to be."*

Shaking her head Stacie said, "Sorry about that mom. Glad you found out before you got involved any deeper with this dirt-bag. You deserve better. I sure hope she beats the hell out of him too. Did you and Susan stay out late? I mean I hope you didn't come home early and stay up all night watching TV. You must have done something since you slept in so late." Christy smiled and said, "I came home early and watched TV for a little while. Then I decided to play a few rounds of Texas Hold 'em poker on my cell phone. I have a guy friend on that game and I was so glad he showed up to play. We played against each other. He really plays well too. We also conversed through instant messaging. It's so refreshing to have a pleasant conversation with a man without all the physical stuff coming into play. Found out we have a lot in common too. But it's just a game and some male company to help pass the time. I'm probably the only other player in the game at his level of play. I sure miss playing poker with your dad. He was really good but I could play as good as him and win my share of matches. In about an hour I was laughing and enjoying the game* *and this guy's company. The bad thoughts brought on by that two-timing Gary were gone. That's why I stayed up late."*

Stacie smiled and said, "I'm glad the whole night was not a loss. But it looks like this guy you met playing poker either does not *have much of a social life or he was in for the night for the same reason you were. By the way, is this guy married?" Christy snickered and said, "He stated that he's single. Don't know if he's telling the truth or not but that's his problem." Looking away, sighing, and picturing what she thought* Clint *looked like in her mind she continued, "I just wanted some decent male company and it was nice. I've played and conversed with him several times this past week. We only know each other by our game names. He goes by the name of 'Clint' and his avatar is a cowboy and I go by the name of 'Pretty Cowgirl' and my avatar is a cowgirl. It's fun and mysterious hiding behind these pseudo-identities. Funny you mentioned that about him. He messaged me that he was in for the night because of a bad experience with a date. I thought it was a strange coincidence but I didn't tell him the same thing happened to me. I told him I was out earlier having dinner with a girlfriend and that I was single too. And yes, I told him I'm straight but I just haven't found the right man!" Rolling her eyes Stacie said, "OK mom. I'm glad you enjoyed the game. I know how much you like to play poker too. Just be careful."*

Snickering she continued, "Now. How about some brunch? I missed breakfast and I'm famished." Christy yawned and stretched her arms, then snickered as she answered, "That sounds great. As long as you're buying. Give me half an hour and I'll be ready."

A little after twelve noon they arrived at the restaurant, sat down, and ordered their food. The conversation was a topic they talked about many times before. "Hey mom," Stacie started. "I've been very concerned about you still being single for eight years now. I know you're searching for someone, but what seems to be the problem with finding a decent guy?" Christy looked around and said, "Decent guys don't wear name tags. *I get hit on so much everywhere I go and it's so hard to tell what kind of a person a guy is just from an opening line and a nice smile. Most of them are wolves like the one from last night. I like to start out as friends and let that relationship take root first before we go anywhere from there. But it's hard to be friends for awhile with a man. Usually they want to hop into bed after* the first hello. *Some of the handsome ones think I want them desperately just because I give them a smile after the once-over look. I find guys these days, no matter what age they are, don't want one woman. They want to* conquer *as many as they can without any commitment whatsoever. I guess other women allow them to do that. I don't know. After last night, I'm giving up for a while. I tried the dating sites like the one you helped me with. But the comments and nasty crap those guys, and some women, posted to me made me cancel my membership."*

Stacie laughed and said, "Yeah, I remember mom. Hey what happened to that guy with the red, green, and blue make-up he had on his face who kept calling on you every time you signed into your site? Remember that creep-o?" Christy's body shuddered as she said, "Did you have to remind me of 'The Face' as I called him? He was scary as hell and would not leave me alone. Even when I took him off my friend list and put a ban on him, he still managed to get through using an alias. I finally threatened to call the police on him. That did not faze him. So I told him I had a cousin who is a mafia hit-man!" Stacie laughed and said, "Did that work?" Christy laughed out loud, "Yep. That did it. He terminated contact with me instantly and I never heard back from him. I looked for him and saw that he closed his account. It was funny to see him run away like a scared rabbit. Anyway, getting back to reality, since you've been gone a lot with work, I've been hoping to find and make friends with a few men, slowly get to know them, and maybe develop a more intimate relationship with one of them. So far they've all been either boring, or wanting to move at the speed of light, or...married like that jerk from last night. I'm going to take a step back and sit on the sidelines for a while and observe. I don't know what else to do."

Stacie thought for a moment then asked, "Mom. Do you think...IF you toned down your looks and maybe dressed a lot more conservative that perhaps guys would look at you differently?" Christy answered, "I tried it. That did not seem to work. I tried to look like a much more conservative woman. I used less makeup and even changed my hairstyle. I think it turned them on more so I gave that up." Stacie responded, "Well mom, you're gorgeous, and I understand why guys are very much attracted to you because you increase their hormone production. I'm gonna tell you what dad told me about guys. He told me that men are born with a brain and a private part, and only enough blood to operate one of those things. He told me to look for guys whose blood flowed north to keep their brains working. Hahaha!" They both laughed. Christy said, "Yes I remember he told me that he thought you were old enough to hear about the birds and the bees. That's too funny. Remember in that same conversation when he told you to stick with the guys who made their decisions with what they had between their ears and not with what they had between their legs? I remember you turned red, squinted your eyes at him, and said, Oh daddy, that's disgusting!"

Stacie blushed and answered, "Oh yeah! That shocked me. I thought the blood saying was going to stay *with me, but the decision making one was the one that got to me and almost made me sick. I told those things to all my girlfriends, and I remember a couple of them told me they told their mothers, and their mothers told them to tell me to stop talking about filthy things like that because I was corrupting them." They both laughed at that as Christy said, "I know. I know. Your dad and I received phone calls from a couple of the girls' parents who told us how bad we were to teach our daughter those things. Your dad laughed at them and told them that their daughters were old enough to get pregnant and one day they will probably find themselves in that situation. So their daughters will eventually have to learn either one lesson or another. Then he asked them: which lesson do you want your girl to learn, and when? One of the parents was angry but the other understood. He certainly had a way of painting a vivid picture of reality to get his point across." Stacie responded, "Yes he did mom. I know we both miss him a lot but with him gone for so long I hate to see you going through life alone. Well, I'm sure we'll think of something."*

Finishing her food first Stacie excused herself from the table to visit the women's room. Passing by the restaurant counter she noticed a sign posted on the window of the store. It read:

> **Enter today to Win an All Inclusive 7 day Bahamas & Grand Cayman Island Cruise for 2 Onboard the**
> ## Atlantic Sun Cruise Ship
> ## "Romance"
> **Featuring Adult Focused Fun, Live Entertainment, and much much more.**
> **Special Feature:**
> **an Amateur Texas Hold 'em Poker Match.**
> **Entry Fee is only $500 per person**
> **1st Prize $15,000 & a Cruise for 2;**
> **2nd Prize $10,000;**
> **3rd Prize $5,000; 4th & 5th Prizes $2500 each.**
> **One entry per person. Call for details.**

Reading this gave Stacie an exciting idea. She thought, 'Wow! I think mom will be thrilled to go on a cruise. She will have a change of scenery, get to meet a lot of new people, and play competitive poker! And...maybe meet a decent man. That's what I'll get her for her birthday present! This is great! She'll love it! Oh my! I'd better get to the bathroom before I wet myself from my excitement.' Rushing to finish her business in the restroom, she came out and stopped by the poster again. She took a picture of it with her cell phone, picked up two entry forms, and headed back to the table.

She stared at her mom with a big grin on her face as she sat down. Christy smiled back and asked,

"OK girl, what's on your mind?" Smiling while answering she said, "Well mom, I was wondering what to get you for your birthday...and I found it! You're gonna flip when you see it!" Christy responded, "My birthday? That's not for a couple of months from now. You found this while you were in the bathroom? I'm not so sure this is gonna be a good thing!" They both laughed at that comment. Then Stacie said, "It was not something I found in *the bathroom. It was something I found* on my way to *the bathroom!"*

Handing her mom an entry form she said, "Here mom. Read the details of this entry form and fill this out for me too so I can enter you into the drawing. I'm going to enter this as well and if I *win I'll take you. But if neither one of us wins I'd like to buy this for you. I wanted to do something special for you and now with my job I can easily afford something really nice like this! What do you say mom?" Stacie was fidgety and nervous as she waited for her mom to finish reading the information about the cruise on the entry form. Seeing her mom smiling and shaking her head up and down increased her excitement, and wanting to say something, Stacie remained quietly seated with her mouth open and her eyes almost bulging out of their sockets.*

Not being able to withstand the suspense any longer of waiting on her mom's response Stacie said, "C'mon mom! What do you think? It looks like it would be so much fun and exciting. We never did anything like this and I know you'll love it." Finally after careful contemplation, Christy looked up at her daughter and said, "Wow! This is fantastic! I never thought of something like this. My friends told me about cruises but I was never one for going passed the sand bar at the beach. I really like it and I've been yearning to play competitive poker for a while now. This is great! Let's do it! And thank you for this great birthday surprise! Brunch turned out to be better than I could have imagined." The two of them kept their smiles and excitement throughout the rest of the time together that day. They had their own thoughts of things to do on the cruise. Before leaving the restaurant each one called their respective employer who cleared them for the time off. After they left the restaurant they drove home and immediately started planning their trip.

In their excitement while they were sitting together at their kitchen table, they realized that they forgot to drop their entry forms into the box at the restaurant. Laughing Christy said, "Well I can drive back and drop them off. It'll only take me about twenty minutes." Stacie laughed and said, "Don't worry about it mom. This is your birthday present from me. I got this. Besides, I never heard of anyone winning anything from those free drawings. *When I read the fine print on the poster it stated that this drawing was for one winner,* from all the entries, from three states." Continuing in a sarcastic manner with a smirk on her face, Stacie said, "Also, it stated that this was done to solicit people to agree to an in-house home improvement marketing campaign, by the same company that tries to sell screened-in room additions for homes. It's a marketing scam. You know how those marketing scams work. Don't you mom?"

Christy gave the same look back at Stacie and sarcastically answered, "Yes I sure do. It's like when a nurse says to a patient's family that she will treat their loved one as if they were one of her own, and then doesn't do it. You know how that goes. Don't you girl?" They laughed as they kidded each other like school girl best friends. They carefully laid out their plans. Stacie called the cruise line company and booked the cruise while Christy researched the ship's layout, the ports of call, and the terms of the amateur poker tournament. After that all they could do was coordinate the things they wanted to do together for their trip. They decided to wait until they were on the cruise before committing to any shore excursions. Their excitement lasted throughout the rest of the weekend.

Chapter 5
Danny's Close Encounter Weekend

Danny *spent the rest of the weekend entertaining friends and family as usual at his home. Saturday afternoon he cleaned the house, and stocked the wet bar with his friends' favorite liquors. He filled the ice buckets and stacked the napkins and glasses in their respective places. He prepared all the hors d'oeuvres and other light snacks. Also, warming in the oven were two trays of lasagna and sitting in the refrigerator were three bowls of Cesar salad. As usual he was very good at providing excellent food and drink for his get-togethers. Just as he was checking on the food and other preparations the doorbell rang. A guest arrived early and took him by surprise.*

"Who could that be an hour and a half early?" he asked himself out loud. Walking to the front door and opening it he said, "Well hello there Maxine. What brings

you here so early? And what did you do with Fred?"
Maxine is the wife of Fred, a bank executive who works
with him. Fred and Danny knew each other from college
and worked together for almost ten years. Maxine was
not an attractive woman. However, in her own mind she
thought she was a ravishing blonde. She was dressed in a
skin tight outfit that less than flattered her appearance,
and only served to emphasize her body's bulging areas.
Danny cringed at the sight. She looked at him and said in
an irate tone, "Fred and I had an argument and I had to
get out of the house. He decided he didn't want to come
over tonight but I always enjoy myself here, and I didn't
want to miss out on the fun. To be honest, Fred is jealous
'cause he thinks I have a crush on you. No matter what I
tell him, he does not *believe me. Even after almost thirty*
years of marriage. I hope I'm not imposing on you by
showing up so early! Am I?"

Taken back by Maxine's confession and showing
up alone made Danny feel awkward and uncomfortable.
Not wanting to rudely turn her out, he decided to let her
in. He hesitated a little as he answered, "No it's not an
imposition at all. It's just a little unusual to see either of
you come here alone. Well, come on in. Do you want to
call Fred and tell him you're here and ok?" That question
irritated Maxine more and she sarcastically answered,
"That won't be necessary. If Fred wants to grow up and
act like a mature adult, he can come here in his own car!

I told him I was coming over, and I was going to enjoy myself." Taken back again by Maxine's answer, he thought a few seconds and said, "Well, ok then. It's early and I can use some help with preparing the food. Or do you want to just sit back and have a drink while I do that?" Maxine smiled as she rocked her head sideways and winked at Danny. Trying to be alluring she answered, "I would love to help you. But how about joining me in a dry martini first so I can get my nerves settled?" He answered, "Sure. I'll mix one for us right now. While I'm doing that, would you please go into the kitchen and turn off the stove? I don't want to burn the lasagna." As she walked past Danny towards the kitchen she answered as sensually as she could, "Ok. By the way Danny darling, make mine a double!" Danny thought, 'Oh shit! That disgusting thing is on the prowl again. Fred told me about her and I've seen the proof with my own eyes too. I don't know why he hangs on to her...I'll fix her wagon.'

Before mixing the drinks, he took out his cell phone, called his daughter Vicky, and told her what was going on as quickly as he could. It was not the first time Danny was alone in the house when a 'cougar wannabe' dropped in on him unannounced. Vicky knew what to do since they used this plan before. Usually he had no problem sending an unwanted visitor away, but this was his friend's wife, and he did not want to be rude, and add to Fred's problems, nor create anything that would bring discord to his work environment. Clicking off his cell phone conversation with Vicky, Danny snickered and thought, 'This is gonna be fun. At least for me. Oh Yeah!' *He smiled as he quickly turned on the video surveillance cameras so he could capture the moment. He did this for two reasons. First, to be sure Maxine did not try to fabricate some sexual crime against him in the probable event of him refusing her advances. And second...just for laughs.*

It took about ten minutes for Maxine to finish checking on the food and turning off the oven before joining Danny in the large open family room, where he was taking his time putting the finishing touches on their drinks. Sitting on a stool at the bar she tried her best to look seductive as she smiled, played with her hair, and winked at Danny as he was shaking the martinis. He fought back the urge to vomit as Maxine smiled and licked her lips at him. He thought, 'Damn she's grossing me out!' Trying to make cute conversation she said, "How handsomely James Bond of you making those drinks. Shaken...not stirred." Fake smiling back at her he said, "That's the only way to make them and enjoy them." With his focus back on the mixture he chuckled as he thought, 'Oh crap! What a turn off. There aren't enough little blue pills, liquor, and paper bags in the whole world, that could make me do what she seems to be thinking I want to do with her!'

As he poured the drinks he looked at Maxine and caught her again trying her best to look sensual, as she licked her lips again, and kept firm eye contact with him. Catching and stopping himself before his body shivered from the heebie jeebies caused by Maxine's nauseating advancing signals he thought, 'What the hell is keeping her? If this witch sticks out her nasty tongue again I'm going to lose it and projectile puke all over that horrific dress she's wearing. What's keeping her?' As he placed the drinks on the counter Maxine reached for her glass quickly to be sure to touch his fingers before he let go. Keeping his repulsion to himself, Danny thought, 'Oh God. Now I'll have to wash my hand in hot lava before I touch and contaminate anything. Thank goodness my tetanus shot has not expired. C'mon Vicky. Hell, where is she!?'

Maxine lifted her glass and was about to make a toast when the doorbell startled her by ringing incessantly. Maxine's expression and demeanor changed as if someone rudely interrupted and stopped her right in the middle of having sex. Sighing quietly to himself Danny smiled and said to Maxine, "I wonder who that could be? People are starting to show up awfully early these days." Putting down his drink, he excused himself as he walked to the front door. Whispering under his breath as he approached the door Danny said, "It's the cavalry...just in the nick of time. What took you so long?"

Opening the door he smiled as he contained his outburst of laughter. In a voice loud enough for Maxine to hear, and with excitement he said, "Oh hello there sexy lady! My you're also early. Come in. Come in. Wow, don't you look terrific!" It was Linda, Vicky's beautiful and voluptuous neighbor and good friend. Linda is in her mid thirties, married with three children, and an ex-swimsuit model who managed to keep her fantastic shape. She was all dolled-up, and like two other times, she was hot and ready to bail him out of another unpleasant situation. She loved playing the part of Danny's 'young gorgeous friend' to help run interference when needed. He thought it was fun, and thought this was going to teach Maxine not to ever come back. Astonished, Maxine's mouth dropped, and her eyes bulged wide open when Linda walked into the room. She thought, 'Oh crap! I can't compete with that!' Trying hard but not even able to keep a phony smile, Maxine was now furious, and thoroughly jealous and embarrassed as she watched Linda putting on her best impersonation of Marilyn Monroe. Danny went into his act as a puppy dog so infatuated with Linda, that it drove Maxine crazy. Back and forth at each other, he and Linda acted like two excited school kids. Watching until she had enough, and with almost a rage about her, Maxine picked up her glass and drank it down. Without delay, she also picked up Danny's glass and drank that down like a sailor at a drinking contest. Glaring at both of them, Maxine stood up, and trying to be rude and insulting she said, "I can see you two need to be alone. If we were in a public place, I'd tell you two to get a room. I'm leaving! I just hope Fred is still at home!" Continuing in a sarcastic tone she said, "Thanks for the drinks, and good night! I know my way out!" Attempting a last jab at Danny and Linda, Maxine forced her butt to shake from side to side as she walked away, not knowing how traumatic it was for him and Linda to watch, as the couple cringed at the sight of Maxine's attempted cat-walk exit.

Sticking to their script, they carried on until a few seconds after they heard the front door slam shut. They waited quietly and patiently until they heard the car engine start. Then, Danny and Linda broke out into side splitting laughter for about twenty seconds. Sitting down at the bar and continuing to laugh between their short comical jabbing comments at Maxine's expense, he opened a bottle and poured Linda a glass of wine. He said, "Did you see the look on her face when you walked in?" In between bouts of laughter Linda responded, "Oh yeah! Her face contorted and went all bulging bug-eyed. I didn't think I was going to be able to hold a straight face. Oh that was too funny! We did this before, but this one was the best. Oh my! Please don't take this the wrong way...but what did she think you were going to do with her? I mean she's not attractive at all! And that outfit was busting out at the seams! I'm not trying to be mean, but a woman her age, and size, ought to know better. And that jiggling butt exit exhibition was a scream! That was a social media video moment that I missed!" Danny said, "At first I was just going to throw her out if she did not stop with her advances. I tried to be decent and push her off gently by not paying her any attention, but that didn't work. That's when I called Vicky to put the plan into play. This woman left her husband, my friend from work, at home and came here early. It was easy to see what she was doing as she basically told me. And I know she has a bad reputation for jumping other men's bones. I figured she needed to learn a lesson. Oh thanks Linda. That was great. I feel sorry for my friend Fred though. But that's something he has to deal with. I don't think I'll see her around here for a long time. What's also funny is...I turned on my cameras so I have this recorded, and from two different angles!" Linda gasped and said, "Holy crap! Can I please have a copy? I have to get this on my social media page and share it!" Danny chuckled as he shook his head and answered, "Oh hell no! I work with her husband, and I don't want any issues whatsoever. I'm keeping this as evidence in case this psycho-witch tries anything stupid. And I do NOT need to have anyone see me on the internet, and associate me with her. I don't need any complications in my life. I'm searching more seriously now for a possible soul mate and I've had enough crazies contact me. I don't need to have lunatics try to chase me down because of a video. Let's keep this between us. I know Vicky and especially Chris will bust a gut laughing at this, but Vicky and Chris are as far as that goes. Ok?" Linda agreed, but still tried to get him to give her the recording. Danny stood firm on his stance. Laughing and enjoying their conversation they waited for the rest of the company to show up, including Linda's husband. The rest of the evening went by with the usual fun and laughter. When the crowd finally filed out of the house Vicky stayed behind to talk to her dad.

"How's it going with the dating site dad?" she asked. Danny shook his head and said, "I'm getting a lot of hits like you told me to expect, but nothing caught my eye yet. I'm going to continue looking. Why don't you come over tomorrow and check it out with me? Maybe you can give me some pointers. How's that?" Vicky gave him a hug before almost walking out the door and said, "Sure dad. And by the way, Linda told me about Maxine's visit. She said you really needed saving from that woman." Danny laughed and said, "Yeah. Linda's a life saver. And dressing up like the knock-out she is, really sent Maxine flying. It was hysterical. And I have the event recorded this time. You'll laugh your butt off when you see it. Let me show you. This is priceless!"

Danny pulled up the recording and watched it with Vicky. They were laughing so hard that she could not hear the conversation in some of the parts. He had to replay several scenes so Vicky could hear what was said. Glued to the screen and between hysterical bouts of laughter, Vicky managed a few comments. She said, "Oh crap! (laughing hard) What the hell is that she's wearing? Oh jeez! And what's with the disgusting lip licking thing? That's gross!" Danny said, "Yeah. And you're watching this on the video screen! Can you imagine what I was feeling like in real time, and as it was directed at me? I almost barfed all over her every time. Now look at what happens when Linda comes in. What a beauty. Keep your eyes on Maxine." Vicky started to comment on Linda then Maxine as she said, "Wow! She's gorgeous. And.......Oh look at Maxine's face! Look at her eyes! (Laughing harder) I have to have a picture of that face. What's she doing now? Looks like she's leaving....Oh NO! Look at her trying to look all sexy as she's walking out of the room. Wow! If she knew what she looks like from behind she would have a cow! I didn't think I could get any more grossed out. (In a sarcastic and joking tone) Hey dad? How about you invite her back and show her this video?" He stopped laughing and sternly looked at Vicky as he answered, "I don't want to see her within ten miles of me ever again!" Vicky said, "I was just poking fun with you, dad. That was really disturbing!"

After shutting off the video, he walked Vicky to the front door. Before she walked out he said, "What's wrong with people like Maxine? I don't understand it and I hope I never do. Anyway good night and I'll see you tomorrow. Drive safe. Love you." Laughing and shaking her head Vicky said, "Dad. I don't know either and I don't want to know why people do the crazy crap they do. I'm very satisfied being normal. Even if normal is not what it used to be in this crazy world. See you tomorrow. Love you too." After another hug and a kiss on the cheek Vicky left. Closing the front door and retiring for the evening, he walked upstairs to his bedroom, turned out the light, and tried to get to sleep. His last thoughts raced to Pretty Cowgirl. He smiled as he imagined that she was, in reality, the beautiful fantasy he pictured in his mind. He thought about opening up the poker game on his cell phone to see if Pretty Cowgirl was playing, but he was too tired and let it go for another night. Then he turned over and within ten minutes he was fast asleep. Meanwhile in Orlando, Florida, Christy was playing poker on her cell phone app and hoping Clint, her online poker fantasy man, was going to join her. After about an hour, she figured he was a no-show for the night. So she shut down her game, and day dreamed about Clint until she fell asleep with a huge smile on her face.

Sunday came and Danny enjoyed the day with Chris, Vicky, and their families. He played with his grandchildren as the others served food, drank, and talked. After a few hours with his grandchildren it was time for them to take their afternoon nap. Danny joined the others and enjoyed the time at the dinner table. There was always something to talk about, and Danny insisted upon seizing these moments with the families. The conversation turned to jokes, events of the past week, and always avoided politics and religion. The main stories that they all laughed with were the stories about Maxine and Peggy. Danny opened up about these two episodes, and his family erupted in laughter as he was animated in his play by play sarcastic description of the events. After the meal everyone except for Vicky left to go home. Chris was going to stick around but he had to get some rest since he had an early morning appointment at work. Vicky's husband Stephen took their child home as Danny was going to drive her home after she finished helping him.

Going into his home office he turned on his computer, and logged into his dating site web page as Vicky joined him with two plates of dessert. She watched as he opened his main page and navigated around the site. First he checked on the comments section to read some of the short messages left for him. There were over two hundred comments left by people who visited his page. All were good and nothing trashy or vulgar from anyone. He read through a few of them before turning to *his daughter and saying, "I guess this section is used by people to help build their self-esteem and self-image before they go on dates. This way, if the date bombs, they can come back to this section, read through the nice comments, and feel better, instead of dropping out off the site. I have to give these people who operate this site credit. These are clever people who know how to work on people's psyche." Vicky shook her head and laughed as she said, "Yep. They make their money with having huge amounts of people registered, and they don't want to lose anyone. Looking at some of these people I believe the website uses its own employees to post something nice. Some of these people are really nerds and weirdoes!" Danny smiled and said, "Ok. Be nice. And remember, beauty is in the eye of the beholder. Even though we know some people need a strong set of prescription eyeglasses." They laughed as he opened the section of his web page that contained messages from people who wanted to chat for a potential date.*

Now both looking at the chat request message and corresponding picture of the person who sent it Danny said, "Ok Vic. Let's see who and what we have here. Hmm hmm. Interesting. Twenty seven women...and eight men." Vicky snickered and jokingly said, "Those are some nice looking guys dad. You sure you don't want to reconsider?" Danny laughed and jokingly answered, "Any more women come around here like Maxine...and that's a possibility. Maybe I ought to send these guys to Fred? That little time around Maxine, I believe, can turn any straight man gay! As for me, I'll thank them for their compliments, and just stick with the ladies. OK?" They both laughed as he sorted through and deleted those he was not interested in by clicking on the 'No Thank You' button beside each request. Reviewing the remaining requests from women in Danny's age bracket, between both of them, they narrowed the field down to four females. All the women in this group appealed to him as far as looks and background. Danny and Vicky researched further into each one's background using popular social media websites. Vicky was very good at finding out about people through these websites. She took over and for each person she researched the internet, and found out a great deal, on other sites, to help him in his date selecting process.

The first one was Cathy, a pretty and fit red head. She stood five foot five and her background was admirable. She is a forty five year old professional in the field of web design. She's divorced, a non-smoker, and likes outdoor activities such as hiking, going to the beach, swimming, and all kinds of other sports. Cathy has no children and lives alone. Vicky was satisfied with her research as she gave Danny a thumbs up. He liked what he saw as well and agreed. One down and one more to go.

The second one was Ruby. Another fine looking red head. Ruby is a forty nine year old woman with a great figure. She has a lot of qualities listed in her profile that interested him. A non-smoker who enjoys cooking and sports. She likes hunting and deep sea fishing which were some of the things he wanted to do more of with a future partner. Vicky then researched her social media websites. Everything looked good except for one thing that caught her eye. There was a link on her social media page with nothing in the link that gave away what the address lead to. What made her curious was the wording above the link that stated: 'Here's a link to an exciting world of my fantasy.' Clicking on that brought up a web page that startled both of them. The link was to a page of people who were hooking up with others. It was open to partner swapping and others who had an 'open marriage.' Danny had a look of disgust on his face as Vicky snickered at what she saw. Danny said, "Now you see why I need you to help me? Look at these freaks!" Vicky said, "Dad? What the hell is an 'open marriage'?" Danny laughed and said, "It's where a married couple agrees to cheat on each other without asking for permission, and not calling it cheating. Kind of a, 'do whatever and whoever you want to do honey,' *kind of thing. This Ruby really gets around. And this website is her way of advertising for more partners. (Laughing) Dump her out of the group now before my computer catches some kind of virus from her. And put a block on* her with the comment, 'I don't swim on another man's beach because I'd probably wind up catching his crabs'." Vicky laughed and said, "Oh dad. That's too funny and probably true. Let's move on."

The third person in the group was Pepper. She was a bronze skinned Brazilian beauty, who stood five foot three inches tall, with a very shapely figure. Another non-smoker who loved to cook gourmet meals, and entertain guests in her home. She claimed she spoke four languages, and worked as an interpreter. Danny and Vicky shook their heads, and were very impressed with her intellectual claims. "Beauty and brains in one package! That's refreshing. Cooks and likes the outdoors. Keep going Vic." While Vicky researched the social media sites she ran into a challenge. "Dad. I'm having trouble finding anything on Pepper. I'm going to try a few other ways using her last name and other items from her profile." Patiently Danny waited until Vicky stopped and said, "Ah ha! Found her. Oh jeez! Look at this dad. Do you see what I see? Take a look at her picture on the dating web page, and look at this one on her social media page. Same person right?" He compared the pictures and the names and said, "How do you like that? Twins from the neck up, and somebody else's body from the neck down." Vicky bit her lip as she shook her head and said, "Yeah. She's a phony. First of all, she's got to be over one hundred fifty pounds heavier in the social media picture.

Second it states that she works as a part time fast food cashier, and is the mother of four kids. Holy shit!" Danny laughed and said, "Man was I almost hooked on that bait. Four languages huh? What a bunch of crap. I feel sorry for those four kids of hers. They deserve a better role model than their mom. Well I'm glad you found this out about her. I can deal with anyone as long as they're honest and truthful. It would have been embarrassing for her if we met and I started speaking one of those languages and she couldn't understand or answer. Dump her too! We're down to the last one. Let's do it."

The fourth person was Simone. A lovely divorced forty three year old brunette and mother of three grown children. With a business degree, she worked in the finance department of a major corporation. Her hobbies were cooking, softball, cycling, and competitive poker. That caught his attention. As Vicky kept up her search, Danny chimed in and said, "How about that? A poker player. She has me at that. What about the social media side? She looks very familiar. I know I've seen her somewhere before. Anything unusual, or is this one a good one?" Vicky scanned the social media web pages and found nothing unusual. She said, "Nothing wild or crazy so far. Five foot eight and looks great in a gown. Finance. Poker. Looks good dad. Should we put Simone on the list?" Danny smiled and said, "Absolutely. Ok. Let's wrap this up and send those two a request for a chat. I can handle it from here. It's getting late and I've got to get you home and get back for a good night's sleep. Don't have a busy week this week, but I don't want to be tired at work. I need to get back to play a couple of hands of poker with my woman poker friend I met on that cell phone poker app I have." Vicky looked up, and smiling she said, "That's pretty cool dad. Who is she?" Danny smiled and said, "I really don't know. We use pseudo names and look for each other when we play. Then we message each other. She's really good at poker. We promised to keep our identity anonymous for now. It's just nice to have her as my fantasy. We have a lot in common regarding things we believe, ideas, politics, etc. It's good for now. If these dates don't work out, I may ask to call on her and exchange phone numbers...and take it slow. Start as friends. Really slow. Thanks sweetheart. You've been a great help. Don't know what I'd have done if I decided to go with Pepper or Ruby. I only know both of those would have been a catastrophe." Vicky completed the messaging, signed off the web site, then shut down the computer. She helped him with the dessert dishes before he left with her to drive her home.

It took about an hour for Danny to arrive back at his home. He opened and entered through the front door, checked all the appliances, took a drink of water, and walked upstairs to his bedroom. After changing his clothes, he brushed his teeth, then took his cell phone and *climbed onto his bed. After finding a comfortable position he sat up and turned his focus to his cell phone. First he checked his messages before tapping the poker game app. Patiently waiting for the game to load, his thoughts raced to his fantasy online poker friend, Pretty Cowgirl. When the game loaded, he went to the section where it listed the friends he 'tagged' during the times he played. Danny selected only people who challenged him, and avoided the ones who played, what he called, 'shit poker.' Scrolling down the list and initially not seeing the friend he wanted to see, he decided to play and hoped that she would join in later. Just then an instant message popped up on his screen. He smiled. It was Pretty Cowgirl just signing onto the game app from her cell phone.*

The message read, 'Hey Clint. Been playing very long? I was hoping you were on so I can have a good challenge.' Not wasting any time he messaged back, 'Hello my Pretty Cowgirl. Looks like great minds think alike. I just signed on myself. Was hoping the same, but not only a challenge, I like the company too. Ready to go a few rounds? Be forewarned. I'm going to play tough.' Christy giggled and said to herself as she typed her messaged, "Come and get it big boy." She sent another message, 'I accept your challenge. Now go for it. Let's see what you got.' Danny smiled and typed, 'You're on!' Both of them were immediately seated at the same table, and started playing. They were excited just to be together, even though they knew very little about one another, other than sharing some of their views on life through messaging.

After about an hour of fairly equal play, he checked the time. Not wanting to stop he messaged Christy, 'It's getting late. I have a lot of work to do tomorrow and have to get up early. Let's call it a draw partner and pick this up tomorrow night.' Christy was thinking the same thing, but glad he brought it up first as she messaged back, 'I could see that I wore you out! Just kidding. I've got to be up early too. Ok partner. It's a draw. But I'm warning you...tomorrow I'm going to clean you out! LOL! (LOL is an acronym used in messaging for Laughing Out Loud.).' Danny messaged, 'It's a date. And bring your A game too. Just so that you can't tell me that I didn't beat you while you were at your best. On a serious note, I really enjoy playing this game and conversing with you.' Christy was touched by Danny's note that she gulped very hard. Not knowing why what he messaged moved her, she got a little choked up. Trying to convince herself it was only a passing fancy, she shook off her emotion and thought to herself, 'It's just a game and I like this guy, but I don't know him!' Typing back she wrote, 'Same here. I really do enjoy playing against you and conversing with you. Very refreshing for me to know there is someone out there that has a lot in common with me. Well, let's call it a draw partner. And thanks for the

good company. Have a good night and sleep well. PC!'
Both of them had a smile on their face as they signed off
the game. After they put down their phones and turned
out their bedroom lights, they laid there in the dark and
dreamt good dreams about one another. Both of them
now having a great fondness for one another, it was a
fantasy they each needed after all the awful dates they
experienced since losing their respective spouse. It took
about half an hour before Danny and Christy finally fell
asleep. Both fell asleep with a smile that only their
imagination knew what it really meant.

Chapter 6
Cathy

The *dates with Cathy and Simone were set up for the following Friday and Saturday, respectively. It was planned to be the same routine which starts with dinner, and if all went well, it would be followed by drinks and dancing at the nearby exclusive member-only lounge. The introductory online chat room discussions went so well with both women, that Danny felt comfortable enough to take it to the next step, and set up the dates. After his embarrassing encounter with Peggy, he made sure NOT to reserve dinner at Lucray's Restaurant with either of these two dates. There were plenty of places he could go that offered a romantic and safe atmosphere, along with excellent food. Work throughout the week was fairly routine, although he ran into Fred several times. There was no mention of Maxine in any of their conversations.*

After arriving home from work on Friday afternoon, Danny showered, shaved, and dressed for his date with Cathy. They arranged to meet at seven p.m. at the restaurant. Stopping by the florist first, on his way to the restaurant, he bought a single red rose for the occasion. This was something of a tradition he started early on with Rachel when they had their date nights. He continued to do this anytime he went on a date with anyone. He even brings a flower to his daughter Vicky, and his daughter-in-law Donna, when they go out for dinner. He found that it was always a great way to set the mood, and all the ladies appreciated it a great deal. He also knew this was something they would always remember about him.

When he walked into the restaurant, he found Cathy sitting at the bar enjoying a cocktail while she waited. She was wearing a very stylish dress. Nothing loud or revealing, but rather very modest. She had a nice shape and didn't need fancy clothes to make her look attractive. He recognized her immediately and thought, 'Well I'm glad she looks like her picture. Pretty face and figure. That's a good start.' She put down her drink and turned her head in the direction of the restaurant entrance, and smiled when she spotted Danny walking toward her. Seeing the rose in his hand, her smile grew larger. Standing up to greet him, they exchanged hellos. When he presented her with the rose, Cathy gave him a short hug and a kiss on his cheek along with telling him, "How sweet that was of you," and, "Thank you for the beautiful rose." The maître'd walked up to them and introduced himself. When he told him who he was, and that he had reservations, the maître'd requested they follow him. Danny waited for Cathy to take her cocktail before walking side by side with her to their reserved table.

The waiter brought them menus and drinks and explained the specials of the day. He and Cathy enjoyed their casual and relaxed conversation as they were getting to know each other. During their conversation he asked, "What do you like and dislike about meeting someone new?" Cathy responded, "I like that it's initially like unraveling a mystery. You know, trying to learn who the other person is. What I don't like is when people try to put on their best face, only to find out later, it's all downhill after that. How about you?" Danny answered, "I like meeting and getting to know new people. I find that casual conversation works best and makes the person feel comfortable. I'm a people person and I find that I'm usually a good judge of character. I use the eighty twenty rule because I'm usually spot on eighty percent of the time. What I don't like is that sometimes first dates are like a job interview. You understand. Many people don't know how to get to know others by simple conversation, so they resort to the one hundred questions. Starting with, 'Where were you born?' and then proceeding to question you from birth through your entire life. I was with a couple of people who, I thought, were going to break out the heat lamp and rubber hose, and interrogate me, as if I were a prime suspect in a crime." his comment made her laugh. Then she said, "That's funny. I've been there too. And I agree. I like the slow casual 'get-to-know-you' conversation. When we chatted online, you made me feel very comfortable. That's why I accepted your invitation for a date."

Dinner and conversation went well. There was nothing negative that either one noticed or felt about the other. After their meal and dessert, Danny felt content and comfortable enough to ask Cathy to join him for drinks and dancing at the Executive Club. She told him she heard good things about that place. Cathy also felt very at ease with him. Enough so to continue on with him to the club. After paying for dinner and walking out to their cars, Cathy got in her car, and followed Danny. At the club they had one drink and danced a couple of dances. All the while they talked, joked, laughed, and got to know more about each other. The music that night was louder than usual, which made it difficult to hold a good conversation. This frustrated both of them. Cathy spoke up and said, "Danny. I do not normally do this, but I feel comfortable enough with you to ask you something. I don't live far from here, and I believe I can trust you to come to my place. It's quieter, and there we can talk without yelling over the music. I can make some snacks, but all I have to drink is red wine. Please forgive me but I don't want you to get the wrong idea about me. I'm enjoying your company, and I want to be able to have a good conversation." He thought it was a great idea and said, "That sounds great. But first, I've got to have a talk with management. This place is not usually this loud. I agree and believe me; I'm not getting any ideas outside of being able to continue with our conversation without the use of a bull horn. I truly appreciate what you're saying, and may I say, I only have respectful intentions. Well. Let's go. And wine and snacks sounds fine with me. Lead the way."

They both stood up and walking toward the exit, Danny stopped to speak to the manager who was holding the door open for them. He asked Cathy to wait outside for a minute while he had a word with the manager. When he joined Cathy outside the club, she noticed he was grinning. She said, "I thought you wanted me out of there for a minute so you could say something that you did not want me to hear. I didn't expect to see you smiling when you came out. What did you say to him?" Danny answered, "You're right. I didn't want you to hear me bless him out. But I did it with diplomacy. I've never let anyone ruin my day, and I'm not going to start any new habits. My company pays a lot of money in memberships and entertainment expenses to places like this. I just told him something he completely understood. And by the way, he asked me to apologize to you too." Cathy snickered and said, "Well I guess he got the message. Listen. I can tell the sound level dropped just after you walked out. That was quick." Danny laughed and said, "Yes it did. I guess he did *get the message..Like the music...(Chuckling) loud and clear. You want to go back in now?" Cathy shook her head no, and laughing she said, "They might turn the music back up if we do. Let's go on to my place and talk some more." He was fine with that since he was actually enjoying this date. He thought as he drove his car and followed Cathy, 'Website dating looks like it has its good points.'*

Parking next to Cathy in the apartment complex parking lot Danny exited his car and joined her on the sidewalk where she led him to her apartment. Walking up to her second floor apartment she unlocked the door. Entering the place, she directed him to the couch where he sat down. Cathy left the room. Danny looked around and waited. The sofa was located in front of the large windows which looked out at the pool. He could hear a group of neighbors enjoying themselves outside at the pool. The pool area was well lit but the curtains did a great job blocking out the light. Cathy entered the room. On the coffee table she placed a glass of water in front of Danny and a glass of wine in front of her where she sat about two feet away from him.

Sitting on the couch, they talked, joked, and laughed for about half an hour. Danny said, "Nice apartment. Do you have any issues with loud neighbors since you're right outside the pool?" Cathy smiled and answered, " Fridays and Saturdays they usually stay out late. They get a little loud but it doesn't bother me." Danny took a sip of water and after putting down his glass he asked, "Tell me Cathy. I'm curious. What interested you enough to agree to a date with me?" Cathy smiled as she tilted her head and answered, " You're handsome, intelligent, down to earth, and you like to have fun. It's my turn. Why did you want a date with me?" Danny looked into her eyes, smiled, and answered, "You're smart, pretty, and in good shape. You seem very energetic and you like to have a lot of fun too."

Cathy smiled as she leaned to Danny and kissed his lips. Leaning back she smiled and said, "Thank you. I wanted to do that since you walked into the restaurant." Danny smiled in response to the kiss and said, "That was nice." Eyeing Danny, Cathy then moved closer to him where her leg touched up against Danny's. In a low seductive tone she said, "I really want to get to know you much better." Again, Cathy leaned in and the couple embraced and kissed passionately. Keeping their embrace after the kiss Cathy rubbed her cheek against Danny's as she let out a lustful sigh and said, "That was much better." Still embraced she pulled back and looking

Danny in the eyes she began to breath heavier as she said with lust in her voice, "C'mon Danny. Let's get more comfortable!" With a lustful smile she let go of her embrace as she stood up from the couch. Standing in front of Danny's face, she quickly slipped off her dress, exposing her sexy body. She was wearing a black sexy lace bra and g-string black panties.

*Danny became very uncomfortable and with some hesitation in his voice he said, "You don't have to do that." With a sensual pout she responded in a provocative sensual tone, "What's the matter Danny? Don't you like me?" Danny smiled and answered, "I like you very much. I just don't know you well enough and I'm a bit old fashion. How about we just sit and talk awhile." Interrupting him was a loud indistinguishable sound that came from the curtain area. Looking there, and then looking up at Cathy he asked, **"What was that?"** Trying to keep her attention on Danny, in a dismissive tone she answered, "It's the neighbors. They probably hit the window with something." Focusing back on Danny, in a seductive tone she said, "Never mind them. C'mon Danny...I find you very exciting and I want you now!" She then quickly put her hands around her bra and with a single motion she ripped off her bra and lunged at Danny as she yelled, **"Take me!"***

Cathy missed Danny as he stood up to avoid her grasp. Suddenly the long set of double curtains crashed to the floor. Inside them scrambling to get out was a naked man holding a video camera. He was taping them. The lights from the pool area shined into Cathy's living room giving everyone a crystal clear view of the action. Standing up and covering his front nudity from Danny, the man was dazed from the fall and didn't realize his naked butt was exposed to the pool party. He stiffened up when he heard the group cheer, wolf whistle, and laugh at him. Lights from the apartment balconies in the background came on. They also cheered and whistled. With all the noise, more apartment lights came on as people came to their windows to see what was going on. Cathy scrambled to cover herself. Danny ran to the front door. Opening it he looked out first to be sure no one saw him before he made a mad dash to his car.

*Entering his car, he made sure all the windows were tightly closed and his car was as sound proof as possible. Cranking up the car he calmly drove out of the apartment complex at first to avoid drawing attention. Then he sped off as fast as he could. Inside his car Danny trembled with anger as he took a sip of water from a bottle he had in his cup holder, gargled with it for a few seconds then spit it out the window. In frustration Danny yelled out the window in the direction of Cathy's apartment, **"Damn freaks! Sick bastards!"** Rolling up his window he let out a few expletives. As he tried to calm down he said, **"Holy shit! What the hell was that all** *about?"* Thinking about it some more he began to laugh hysterically.

Calming down enough to think rationally, he picked up his phone and called Vicky. Answering on the third ring she said, "Hey dad. It's early. Let me guess. Your date with Cathy didn't go well either!" Answering in a controlled angry tone he said, "Let me say that my date with **Peggy** was safer and more enjoyable! **I'm lucky I escaped before anyone went to jail!**" Concerned and surprised Vicky asked, **"Jail? What happened?"** Danny grumbled and sarcastically answered, **"Lights, camera, action!"** Confused with his answer Vicky asked, "What?" Danny answered with contained anger and frustration, **"THEY, are a bunch of freaks?"** Confused and trying to help understand Vicky asked, **"Calm down dad. What's going on and who's THEY?"**

He paused as he huffed and sighed in frustration. Then answering in a sarcastic tone as he laughed he explained, "The club was too loud for us to hear our conversation so we went to Cathy's apartment. At first things got a little romantic and nice. Then suddenly she went into **ape-shit wild beast sex mode!** She stood up, threw off her clothes and tried to jump my bones! Just as I backed off, the **shit hit the fan!** Vicky asked with anticipation, "What happened then?" Danny laughed hysterically before calming down and answered, **"Her boyfriend who was hiding behind the drapes with** *a video camera fell and took all the drapes down with him. He was butt naked. Everyone in the apartment complex, especially the pool party right behind him, saw everything. They were whistling, cheering, and screaming."* Laughing out loud she asked, *"What did you do?"* Wiping his eyes from tears of laughter Danny answered, *"I got my ass out of there before anyone saw me. I didn't want to stick around to star in some porn film!"*

Now he could hear not only Vicky but Stephen laughing hysterically as well in the background. Danny now also laughing loudly said, *"Hello Stephen. I guess I'm on speaker and you heard."* Stephen sat up in bed. Unable to speak he held his stomach, laughed, then laid back down in bed. Laughing through her conversation with Danny Vicky replied, *"He can't answer right now. He's laughing too hard!"* Danny sighed and said, *"I knew internet dating was dangerous. If Simone doesn't work out...I'm done with it! I'm going home and playing online poker. It's safer!"* Vicky laughed as she wisecracked sarcastically, *"I understand dad. Just one question: When is the movie 'Danny Does Cathy' coming out in theaters?"* Danny chuckled as he replied, *"I was waiting for your wise ass remark. Okay, good night honey. (louder) Goodnight Stephen!"* Vicky and Stephen laughed as they replied, *"Goodnight dad!"* Danny laughed as he tapped his phone to end the call.

Driving home, he focused on Simone, his next date, and tried to put this one behind him. After arriving home, he checked all the appliances in the kitchen, set the house alarm, and went upstairs to his bedroom. Too tired and frustrated to do anything else, he changed his clothes, brushed his teeth, climbed into bed, turned off the light, and closed his eyes. Before falling asleep he said out loud, **"I hope Simone is nothing like Peggy or Cathy!"**

Chapter 7
Simone

Saturday *morning Danny decided to sleep in until ten a.m. He planned to take most of the morning to rest before going to the gym in the afternoon. After washing up, making coffee, and a small breakfast he sat in his bedroom. Turning on the TV set he watched the news. Not liking what he saw he shut it off, and decided to play a few hands of poker on his phone app. Soon after logging into the game and playing a few hands, he was pleasantly surprised, and he smiled as he read a message directed to him. It read, 'What's the matter Clint, got no friends? LOL!' It was from Pretty Cowgirl. If the coffee didn't get him motivated, her presence online surely did the trick. He replied, 'Looks like you're in the same boat as I am! Where's the crowd around you these days? LOL!' She replied, 'Just kidding of course partner. Taking it easy today and being a little lazy before I get up and go to the gym. Nice to sleep in once in a while.' Danny laughed as he messaged back, 'Doing the same exact* *thing here. Getting a much needed mental health break this morning before heading out to the gym this afternoon. Gotta stay in shape to compete with you. Great minds think alike. Glad to know you like to stay in good condition.' His message was more than just being glad she is exercising. He wanted to see if Christy was going to elaborate on her figure. He got his answer when she replied, 'Absolutely. I like to stay fit and in good condition. There's nothing like a good high feeling from all those endorphins after a good workout. How about you?' Now Christy was fishing for some more information about this mysterious man. And she got her answer when he replied, 'Been fit and in excellent shape and condition since I was a teenager and I do NOT plan on letting myself go either. That's great. Now, let's see if we can wear each other out with a few hands of Texas Hold 'em. Ready partner?' Christy smiled and replied, 'Anytime you are. Bring it on my man! LOL!' Reading that Danny said to himself, "Ooo! My man huh? Well that sounded nice. I like her style."*

It was noon before Danny and Christy finally called it quits for the day. Again, Christy was very competitive, and they were both very content with the play and the conversation during the games. This time though, after the game and before signing off, Christy requested that they set up a time to play again on Sunday night. It was the first time during their time playing together that they set up a 'poker date.' From their conversations, and with their fantasies about one another, they were developing unusual feelings for each other. Both of them thought the same thought when they logged off the game, and put their cell phones away. Each thought, 'This is weird. I know so little about this person, and yet I'm starting to feel an attraction, and develop some feelings for him/her. Strange! Very strange!'

It was almost four p.m. at the gym when he finished his workout, showered, and headed home. He took his time and relaxed for a couple of hours before dressing, and leaving for his date with Simone. As usual he picked up a single red rose before driving to his favorite Italian restaurant for dinner. Upon entering the fine restaurant about fifteen minutes early, he was greeted by Mario, the host and owner, who knew Danny over the years when he used to frequent his establishment with Rachel. Mario greeted him with a big smile and a strong handshake. Then he led him to a reserved table where Danny had an excellent view of the restaurant entrance. Mario made sure the waiter brought him his favorite cocktail while he waited. Then he lit a tall red candle, and placed it in the middle of the table. Within about five minutes his date, Simone, arrived. She was standing at the front of the restaurant waiting for the host. Danny looked up and smiled as he saw a stunning woman in a long elegant gown that had a slit halfway up her right leg, revealing a nice looking firm, but shapely, and muscular leg. He thought to himself, 'Wow! Very nice! Tall, pretty, and nice figure. This is going to be interesting.'

Spotting Danny, Simone smiled, and did not wait for Mario to come escort her. Simone walked directly to the table. Exchanging hellos, Danny presented her with the rose, and waited for her to be seated before taking his seat. Mario came to the table to offer his apologies for his tardiness in attending to his duties as a host, along with bringing her a glass of Chablis. With a grin on his face, Mario said with a heavy Italian accent, "This a one is on da house Madam Simone. Enzo will be here in a few minutos to take your order. Enjoy your dinner." Turning to leave, Mario looked at Danny, smiled and winked. After they greeted and introduced themselves, the couple talked for a few minutes before the waiter came and took their order.

During dinner, along with the general discussion that came with meeting someone new, Danny asked, "So you know Mario? Do you come here often?" Simone smiled and answered, "Yes. I've known Mario for years. I used to come here frequently with my family before my divorce. Now it's usually just me and a friend. His food is excellent. Very authentic. He's such a sweet man, and always takes great care of his patrons." Danny *agreed and said, "Yes, he's a good guy. I used to come here with my family quite often before my wife passed away. I shied away for a while afterwards. I was trying to avoid places that brought up a lot of memories. It took a while, but I'm over a lot of that stuff. Still have some sentimental moments though. But I've learned to deal with them." Changing the subject he asked, "Is your food alright?" Smiling and feeling empathy for him, Simone said, "The food is always great, and I understand what you mean. After my divorce, I went through a lot of emotional turmoil during my transition. Going from married, and family, and all that goes with it, to single life is a huge challenge, and can get the best of you if you let it. Like you, I learned to deal with **all** the changes in my life too."*

About an hour later, they finished their meal, and were almost done with their wine. From their conversation, they learned much more about each other. They really had a lot in common. Looking at Simone, Danny thought for a moment and said, "Looking at your pictures online I could swear we've met before. Now, seeing you in person, I still believe we've met somewhere before. Did you get that same feeling? I've been racking my memory banks trying to figure it out." Simone smiled and said, "I know I've seen you before as well. Maybe later it will come back to you. But for now, let's talk some more." Danny laughed as he said, "Besides also being in finance, one of the things that got me when I read through your hobbies, is that you like to play competitive poker. That's my game too, and I play competitively every chance I get at the casinos in several states. Where do you normally play competitively?" Simone laughed and said, "I normally play with friends from work. We have a group of twenty people, and we get together every two months or so, and play elimination matches until we get down to five people, who split the pot at the end. It's our way of playing like they do on that TV sports channel. It's a lot of fun, and the pot is usually around a thousand dollars split amongst the five according to their final rank. It's exciting and everyone really enjoys it." Danny said, "That's very interesting. I like that. I usually play with people from work and some acquaintances, but we never set up something like you described. I'm going to pass the idea of the way your games are set up and see what my poker buddies say. That really is a great way of playing. Thanks for telling me. It sure will make it more interesting." Finishing their drinks Danny asked Simone if she would like to extend the date, and go with him to an upscale club. Simone was very pleased and accepted. This club was about twenty miles away on the other side of town. He did not want to take a chance going to the same club he took Cathy, and potentially deal with loud overbearing music. This club catered to an older crowd, and played softer mellow tunes, particularly for couples to slow dance.

Simone knew the place too, and driving her own car, met Danny there forty minutes after leaving the restaurant. It's been a long time since he was there, but the place had not changed. The music was at a volume where people didn't have to talk loudly to hear each other. Ordering drinks, Danny and Simone stuck with wine. For about forty five minutes they talked, laughed, and joked. Mainly about their hobbies, and their experiences with poker matches. He still had a feeling he met Simone somewhere before. Sometimes during their conversation, he stared at Simone's face, neckline, and all the way down her arms to her hands. There was something familiar. Finally he gave up since he thought he was trying too hard and did not want to lose his chain of thought with their conversation. Then an old familiar slow song started to play that they both liked very much. Simone accepted Danny's request for a dance, and the couple walked to the dance floor where they embraced as they began to dance. About half way into the song the couple went from smiling and looking into each other's eyes, to pulling in closer and now dancing cheek to cheek. That felt good to both of them.

Dancing closer together, Danny thought, 'Simone's got a firm body. Nice strength in her hands. She must really work out a lot to stay in this good a shape.' Simone now feeling excited about being in his arms, pulled him in closer. Their bodies were now firmly *against each other. Feeling better and being this close together with their bodies rubbing up against each other aroused Danny. He thought, 'Oh crap. I'd better start thinking of baseball or something before I embarrass myself.' As Simone began to gently blow into Danny's ear, the thoughts in his head reached the World Series highlights. Keeping his thoughts on the ballgame and his attention on the embrace during the dance, Danny gently rubbed his hand in a caressing manner across Simone's lower back. This made Simone let out a few short moans of excitement between blowing in his ear. Suddenly, Danny stopped as he felt a very unusual sensation from Simone's body. He thought, 'What the hell is that?!' Simone pulled away a little and smiled at Danny. Simone snickered and said, "Sorry Danny! I tried to control myself but I could not help it!"*

Luckily for Danny the club had low lighting, so it was dark enough for others not to notice. Danny was now containing his anger as he calmly asked, "Is that what I know it is?" Simone answered, "Yes it is." Danny broke off the embrace, and as nonchalantly and cool as he could, he lead Simone away from the dance floor and back to a table as far away from everyone that he could find. Sitting down across from one another, Simone could tell Danny was angry. Contained anger, but angry none the less. Danny thought a moment before speaking. He was trying his hardest to be cool, but at the same time to get to the point. He looked at Simone and said, "You owe me a huge explanation! With all due respect, why didn't you tell me during our chat that you are what you are? You owe me that much! Go ahead. I'm listening!"

Simone took a deep breath and said, "I'm not ashamed of who I am. I do apologize for not telling you during our chat, but I was afraid you wouldn't want me." Danny interrupted, "You got that right! Go on!" Simone continued, "Well you were so gentle, sweet, intelligent, and kind, that I wanted to be with you. Actually I wanted to be with you for several years, and I finally took the chance when I found you online on the dating website." Danny straightened up in his seat, and with a look of confusion he asked, "What? Several years?! Oh shit! I knew it! I knew I've seen you somewhere before. How do you know me, and who are you really?!" Simone answered, "I'm...Bob from the accounting department. I've worked down the hall from you for almost eight years before taking a job with another bank." Danny sighed hard and slapping his thigh said, "Holy crap. Bob! Molly's husband! But what's with all this Simone stuff? When did this happen?" Simone answered, "Well I just could not go on any longer. I revealed myself to Molly...But she did NOT take it very well. She threw me out of the house, took the kids, and moved back to Bismarck, North Dakota. I'm sorry, and I hope I didn't make you angry. I really like you...A lot. You were always good with everyone, and you're such a beefcake that I...well I did what I did. Sorry you don't like what I did."

Danny looked at Simone and said, "Hey look. First of all I think I can appreciate what you're saying, and I think I should thank you, IF that was meant as a compliment. But I value honesty. If this is what you want, you're a grown ma....Oops. Sorry. A grownup. However, what you have is not what I desire, and I hope you understand that. That's not my preference. I mean you actually look terrific, and nothing like what I remember Bob looked like! You fooled the hell out of me up until the time on the dance floor where I got to know you much better than I would have liked to that is!"

Danny thought a second, and his jaw dropped as he recalled something earlier. He said, "Oh damn! Now I understand why Mario smiled, and winked at me in the restaurant. Of course he knows who you are! So that's what you meant when you said transition!" Simone snickered and said, "You should have seen the expression on Mario's face when he saw me for the first time after my transition. (Chuckling) It was priceless! He didn't know what to do. His jaw stayed dropped the whole time. He kept bowing and apologizing. After I told him, he stayed in a state of total confusion. He kept calling me 'BobSimone' and apologizing. He even brought the cooks out to see me. They didn't know, so at first they looked at me like I was eye-candy. Then they looked terrified after

Mario explained to them in Italian who I was before. I kept catching them trying to look down my cleavage. I could not help myself. I had to laugh every time."

Out of pure curiosity they talked a little longer because he wanted to know more about Simone's transition. Danny was not the kind of person to get really angry, and tear into someone just because he felt like it. He exercised great self-control. After talking about working at the bank, Danny decided to end the conversation, and leave, alone and separately. Standing up he smiled at Simone as he extended his hand. Shaking hands and saying goodbye, Danny told Simone he was not going to make any more contact with Simone in the future, and would keep this to himself. He asked to leave first and as he stood up from the table Danny looked around to be sure no one was watching them before quickly heading for the exit. Getting into his car he cranked it up and left the area as fast, and as inconspicuous as he could.

It was eleven o'clock while driving home. Danny felt numb inside as he thought about the experiences from this dating site. At that point he felt like deleting his account and never doing any kind of dating online ever again. He then decided he needed a change of scenery. To take a break and get away for awhile. He had a vacation coming up and wanted to go somewhere.

...Anywhere. About twenty minutes before arriving home, he decided to call his daughter.

Speed dialing her number he waited for her to answer. She answered on the fourth ring, "Hey Dad." He said, "Hey hun." Vicky replied quickly, "It's early. Don't tell me! Let me guess. This date didn't go well either. What happened?" Danny answered, "First, take me off speakerphone. I don't want anyone else to hear this. OK?" She answered, "Sure dad. Stephen is upstairs. I'm downstairs putting away some things. No one else can hear." Danny said, "Good. I don't want anyone else to know this. Well! You won't believe it! You won't believe it...because I still don't believe it! You ready for this?" She said, "Yeah. I'm sitting down." Danny said, "Good. I was going to tell you to sit down too. (Deep sign) Here it goes...Simone...is NOT Simone!" In a concerned voice Vicky asked, "What? If Simone is not Simone...then who is she?"

Danny chuckled as he said, "Hold on tight! Remember when I told you I knew I saw Simone somewhere before? Well I was right. Simone is really...Bob from accounting! **Get that?** *Bob from Accounting is now Simone! What a kick in the head! You there? Hello? Hello? Vicky? Did I lose you?" Vicky came back on laughing, "Sorry dad. You didn't lose me. I put the phone on mute so you wouldn't hear me laughing. Bob!? Oh crap dad. The same Bob that used to come over* *with his wife Molly, and played poker with you and the guys?" Danny said, "Yes. That Bob. It seems he made some **big** changes in his life." Vicky still laughing said, "That's wild! How did you find out?" Danny laughed and snorted as he explained, "I didn't know until we were at the club and decided to have a slow dance. Things between us got a little hot and Simone became a bit too excited and could not hide the effects of the excitement as she danced the 'hokey pokey!' Shocked the living hell out of me! I stopped and stepped back, and lead Simone off the dance floor and to a table, way the hell at the back of the place, and demanded an explanation."*

Vicky was again holding her stomach and laughing while her phone was on mute to avoid her father from hearing her. He continued, "You have me on mute again? I know it's funny as hell to you. To me it's another, 'what-the-hell' moment! Oh, and by the way, I won't be going back to that Italian restaurant for a long time. Mario, the owner, knows ALL about BobSimone, as he calls Simone."

Vicky controlled her laughter as she asked, "Well. What are you going to do now, dad? I mean, I can't blame you if you don't want to use that online dating service anymore, seeing how all the dates were disasters." Danny answered, "I was thinking of that before I called you. I have some vacation time coming up and I'm gonna take a huge break and get away. Change of scenery and all that. I don't know where yet but I'm getting the heck out of Dodge for a while." She responded, "I can really understand what you're saying and I think you're ready for something like that. How about if we talk about this tomorrow during dinner with the families? I'm sure we can brainstorm and come up with something. What do you think, dad?" Danny said, "One condition! You do NOT mention ANYTHING about Simone, or Bob, or anything of what we just talked about. If anyone asks, just tell them it didn't work out, and leave it that way. NO other details. Capeesh?"

Vicky laughed and said, "Yes, dad. Don't worry. I totally understand. Just one last question. Did you kiss Simone?" Danny answered, "You never disappoint me! I was waiting for your smart-ass remark. The answer is NO, I did not kiss Simone. But I laughed when I thought about what I would say if I ever ran into Simone again. I would ask BobSimone: Is that a pencil in your pocket, or are you glad to see me?! Hahaha!" He could hear Vicky laughing hysterically with that comment. She said, "Dad. That's too funny. Anyway, sorry this online service didn't work out. Wait a minute. I have an idea. How about introducing Simone to Fred? I mean you never know. He might find Simone better than Maxine! Hahaha! Ok Goodnight dad. Love you!' Danny laughed and said, "Now that's an idea. Ok hun. Goodnight. Love you too. See you tomorrow."

Chapter 8
Danny's Getaway Plan

Arriving *home after his date with Simone, Danny entered his house, loosened his tie, poured himself a couple of ounces of eighteen year old scotch, sat in his living room easy chair, and sipped it slowly as he thought about living the rest of his life alone. He was not having a pity party nor was he feeling depressed. It was time he needed to think as he was unwinding before going to bed. A few minutes later, he smiled as he stood up, and walked to the kitchen as he finished his drink. He was thinking about Pretty Cowgirl, and hoping she was going to be playing tonight as well. They arranged a time on Sunday night to meet up and play but he needed to have contact with her tonight for his own sanity. Hurrying up to his bedroom, he changed clothes, and washed before getting into bed, and logging into his cell phone's poker app. Holding his breath as he checked the list of his tagged friends currently playing, he smiled from ear to ear when he saw Pretty Cowgirl on the list. Clicking on her name, he joined the table where she was playing. He thought as* *he exchanged messages with her, 'Whoever the heck you really are, I don't care. For now you're a great distraction and a great fantasy for me. God I hope if we ever meet that you're as great as I imagine you are.' Laughing and joking they exchanged jabs at each other such as, 'It's after two a.m. Don't you have a life?', and, 'What's wrong? Still don't have any friends?'*

They played and exchanged jabs, humor, and appreciation for one another for about two hours before calling it off. Before leaving the game, Christy sent Danny some surprising messages. They read, 'Well cowboy. I'm glad I met you. Even if it's online and behind the veil of anonymity. Maybe someday we can open up and reveal our true identities. But for now and for my own reasons I like it this way. Hope you understand. Thanks. I enjoyed the game and always enjoy your company. See you tomorrow night! (turning sarcastic) And get some sleep! You're gonna need it to play at my level. LOL! Goodnight my sweet Clint.'

He couldn't believe what he read. This pumped him up which now made him wide awake. He thought, 'Damn! I needed that! I need to respond before she signs off.' Quickly he messaged, 'Hold on a second partner.' He needed a little time to think about his response. Typing as quickly as he could he messaged, 'You really made my night with your last comments! I feel the same about enjoying your company. Very refreshing in light of some of the people I've met lately. I agree also about the anonymity. I too have my own reasons to keep it anonymous. I look forward to opening up someday. But for now I also want it this way too. Sort of an escape from reality with a private friend on our own private island in my mind. I'm glad we met too. Ok my sweet cowgirl. (turning sarcastic) Enough of that mushy stuff. We both better get some rest or we'll be passing out during the game. Hope you have some great dreams...About me! LOL! Goodnight.' Getting a last jab in there Christy messaged, 'I plan on some great dreams about you...about beating the heck out of you and taking all your chips the next time we meet. LOL! Thanks Clint. Til then. I'm your Pretty Cowgirl.' After logging off and putting away their cell phones, Danny and Christy again, laid in bed with smiles on their faces while fantasizing about being together until finally falling asleep.

At eleven a.m. a phone call from Chris awakened Danny out of a sound sleep. Answering in a groggy voice he said, "Hey Chris how's it going?" Chris answered, "Just fine, dad. Did I wake you up?" Chuckling, Danny answered, "No. The phone woke me up! I was up for a while last night and didn't fall asleep until after four this morning." Chris responded, "Wow! You must have had a really nice time on your date with Simone to stay up that late! I know what I did on my dates with Donna when we stayed up that late! Good going dad. Are you gonna tell me about it later?" Danny shook his head as he answered, "Let's not discuss that please. It's not what you think or even close to what you're picturing son! And NO! I was not with Simone that late. As a matter of fact I terminated my date early last night, and I don't plan on having any future encounters with Simone. I will talk to you later about that, and only to you. Privately. I'm not gonna discuss this on the phone. Ok? Sorry if I'm a little short with you, but I have my reasons and I'm tired right now." Chris responded, "No problem, dad. Well, since you didn't get much sleep, are we still on for dinner later?" Danny answered, "Of course we are. I need my fix of time with my family. That's what keeps me going. It's the best and only drug I do. Without you guys, my life will lose its meaning. Especially in light of my catastrophic attempts at meeting a new life partner. So I'm gonna take a break from dating for a while. I talked to your sister last night, and I'm glad you called 'cause I wanted to talk to you too. I'm going to take some time off and get away. You know. Change of scenery and all that, for about two weeks, and I need you guys to brainstorm with me on what to do and where to do it. Think about that, and we can talk later. Right now I'm going to get up and take a shower. Ok?" Chris answered, "Sure dad. I'm sure we can come up with some great ideas. Sorry things haven't been working out for you. Ok then. We'll see you around five o'clock. Bye for now." Danny said, "Great. I'm looking forward to some R *and R away for awhile. Thanks son. See you and the family later. Love you. Bye!" Terminating the call, he got out of bed, went to the kitchen to turn on the coffee maker, then went to the master bathroom and showered.*

At around five o'clock Danny's son and daughter arrived with their families. Greeting his grandchildren first, he got his fill of baby hugs and kisses. That gave Danny the fulfillment he needed to pick him up for the rest of the week. Next he greeted Donna and Stephen, then his son Chris and daughter Vicky with hugs and smiles as usual. Filling his house with all kinds of sounds from talking, to the grandkids whining and crying, always gave Danny pleasure. It was a routine Sunday family get together. Having a few drinks, playing with the grandchildren, talking about all kinds of subjects, and preparing the main meal, was always a special time for him.

The first chance he got, he pulled Vicky aside and reminded her to be absolutely silent about his date with Simone. She looked at Danny and asked, "Simone who?" He smiled and winked acknowledging his appreciation for her silence. Dinner was served at seven thirty as the conversation moved to the dining room table. They gathered around and said a prayer before eating. Dinner was pretty routine. They ate, told jokes, laughed, and talked mainly about superficial topics like sports, news, and what the grandkids did during the week.

During dessert though, Danny broached the subject of his recent dating results. Not speaking on anything specific he avoided provoking any uncomfortable comments. What I want to say is, as you know, I'm going to take a break from the dating scene. I plan on taking some time to get away from here for a while too. What I requested from Chris and Vicky was to brainstorm, and come up with some suggestions. What I'm trying to do is get away from work, and see or do something different. This has nothing to do with my family. I love all of you, and these times together are sacred to me." They all understood, and then the suggestions started to pour out of all of them.

Danny said, "Hold on a minute. Looks like you guys did a lot of thinking about this. One at a time please, and give me your top choice of ideas. I'm going to be taking mental notes here. Donna spoke first, "Well dad. I think maybe you should do something exotic like a trip to the South Pacific island of Fiji. I looked it up, and the place is absolutely magnificent. Beautiful waterfalls, lots of activities like fishing, and scuba diving, and crystal clear ocean beaches." Danny said, "Yes. That sounds great. Rachel and I had a trip to Fiji on our bucket list. I'm familiar with the scenery you're describing. I like the sound of that. Thanks Donna. Ok. Next...Chris?" Chris said, "I thought about you doing the African Safari tour. If that's not a change of scenery and get away, then I don't know what is. I researched it, and it's very reasonable, and can fit your time frame." Danny shook his head and said, "I thought about that, and I appreciate the suggestion. But this time around I'm thinking that's something I'll put off until we can do that together. We talked about it before. Next. Vicky. What did you come up with? Vicky said, "I did a lot of thinking dad, and all I could come up with is, to do something from the bucket list that you and mom made up. I figured those were the things you really wanted to do and I wanted you to look there first." Taking a teasing jab at her he responded, "Aha! You took the easy way out, didn't you? Just kidding hun. That's a good thought. Ok. We saved the best for last right Stephen?" Stephen smiled as he said, "That's right dad. I found something absolutely by accident when I was searching online. We all know how you love to play poker, and how you have not played in a tournament since Rachel. Well I found something that includes an exotic change of scenery too. It's a seven day cruise to the Bahamas, and Grand Cayman Island, that features an amateur championship Texas Hold 'em poker match with a fifteen thousand dollar first prize." Handing Danny a printout of the details, Stephen continued. "Here's the information I printed out from the cruise company's website. It's on the Atlantic Sun Cruise ship named Romance. What do you think?"

Danny looked over the information, and before he could say anything Vicky spoke up and said, "Wow! That sounds great. I'd like to go on that one myself." Stephen looked at Vicky and said, "If your dad wants to go, and wants company, then go ahead. Between me and the rest of my family, and Chris and Donna, if they can, we can take care of our son." Looking back at Danny he asked, "What do you think dad?" Danny was studying the information. He thought for a moment to consider everyone's ideas before looking up and saying, "I love everyone's ideas. But the one that really won me over is Stephen's. I like that one the most of all. And yes, *I've been craving to play some competitive poker for a few years now. And I really like this cruise idea as a getaway bonus. How about it Vicky? Want to accompany your dear 'ole dad? We can have separate rooms."*

Turning to her husband she said, "Thank you honey!" Vicky turned and smiled at her dad and said, "Sure! I'd love to go with my dear 'ole dad. That sounds like a lot of fun, and if you meet someone, I can work with you to spy on them since everyone is confined to the ship. Hahaha!" Danny said, "That's great. And thank you for coming with me Sherlock! I could use an extra pair of eyes in case we run into another cat-woman or any other kind of wild woman!" *They all laughed at Danny's comment, but only Vicky knew what he meant by* 'any other kind of wild woman.' *Then they raised their glasses* to toast to Danny's success on the cruise, and in unison they said, "Cheers!"

Later on that night after everyone went home, we find Danny preparing for his poker game with Pretty Cowgirl. Sitting up in bed he waited until it was time to log into his phone's poker app and join Pretty Cowgirl for their first poker date. Entering the game's main page, he clicked on the friends list. And there she was in the 'tagged' friend list. Within a few seconds he received an invitation from her to play a private game. Tonight he felt his heart beating faster with the excitement of getting together with her. Christy was excited too. They both still did not understand their feelings. Not wasting any time he accepted her invitation and was immediately joined with her in the game. For the first time it was only the two of them at their own private table. The app allowed players to setup private games and have other players join them by invitation only.

Danny messaged, 'Hello my sweet Pretty Cowgirl. So glad to be with you again. How are you tonight?' Christy responded, 'Great. I was actually excited about playing with you tonight.' Re-reading what she wrote she laughed and quickly corrected herself, 'I mean playing against you tonight. Sorry. Lol! How are you and did you get any rest?' Danny smiled at her comment and correction, and messaged back, 'Freudian slip? I hope. Lol! Yes. I got some sleep. No excuses *though. Rest or no rest I always play to win.' She smiled and messaged back, 'Same here. If I'm in it, I'm in it to win it. No excuses. Before we play though, I wanted to ask you something.' Danny messaged, 'Shoot partner. What's on your mind?' The next messages stunned Danny. Feeling somewhat scared she messaged, 'I did a lot of thinking from our last conversation and I'm taking a chance saying this and I hope I don't scare you away. Well here it goes. I don't know why but I'm really starting to like you a lot. It's strange and I can't explain it. Someday down the road I would like to get some more information about you and maybe exchange numbers and have a phone conversation. In the meanwhile I want to take it slow. I have a lot of personal things to do and I want to be sure of what I'm feeling. Does that sound crazy?'*

He could feel his heart beating harder in his chest again. For the first time he wanted to go a bit faster but caught himself before he sent the wrong message. He typed, 'That's not crazy at all. It's been a very strange experience for me as well. There were times during our conversation that I found myself thinking about the same thing, and I didn't want to scare you away either. I agree and I too have some personal and work related things I have to do. I'd like to keep things like this for a couple of months. At least until I get back from my trip. After that, if we still feel the same, I would really like to call you and talk. What do you say?'

Christy was elated that he was feeling the same as she was. Her heart was pounding too from anticipating the eventual revealing of the mysterious person she only knew as 'Clint.' She messaged, 'Thank you so much my friend. I've never felt like doing this with anyone before, in an online game, over the internet. I hear there are so many strange people you run into. But I don't feel that way about you. It still boggles my mind. You understand what I'm saying, right?' Danny thought to himself, 'I know it firsthand sweetheart!', as he messaged back, 'Yes I truly understand. And I too sense a great feeling about you. I know a lot about meeting people online and the kind of people you can run into. Someday I may just share a few interesting stories of my own with you. Anyway I'm so glad we got that out on the table. No pun intended. How about we just call it a night for now? After our discussion here, I'm feeling good, but I'm really not in the mood for competitive play. After what we told each other, I don't feel like I want to beat you and take all your chips. Lol!'

Messaging back Christy typed, 'Me too. I feel sort of vulnerable now that I let my guard down. You're just so easy to talk to. I really liked how you put it last time. My private friend on our own private island in my mind. Anyway, I really appreciate your honesty, and I'm glad you're still here. And I'll be back again and ready to take you to Boot Hill. Lol! You have a good night's sleep and we'll catch up again another night. Goodnight my sweet cowboy.' Danny smiled and messaged back, 'You caught me completely off guard tonight. I'll catch up with you again so get ready for a good ole fashion tail kickin' next time we have a showdown. Lol! Good night, and Thanks my sweet Cowgirl. Sweet dreams! And you can bet the farm that I'm going to have some nice dreams tonight partner!' Smiling, Christy ended with the message, 'You can count me in too! Yahoo and goodnight!' Signing off the game app it took both of them about an hour before their excitement calmed down long enough for them to focus on getting to sleep.

During the week, between work, working out at the gym, and routine things to do at home, Danny and Vicky planned their trip. They got together on Wednesday night to go over all the details. They re-verified their passports were valid, secured their vacation time off from their respective employers, called the cruise company's main office, booked and paid for two ocean view cabins for the October 29th sailing from Miami, Florida. Danny then called several of his poker buddies to help him organize three Texas Hold 'em tournaments, Simone style. Playing under the same conditions as described in the cruise company's website were the same ones described to him by Simone of elimination matches with a maximum of twenty players.

He was pleasantly surprised that they were able to get more than twenty players immediately. With a fifty dollar buy-in, making it a one thousand dollar pot, split by the last five players, that was not only very affordable but very appealing. What appealed to Danny was that there were players attending whom he never played against. He thought, 'Well, the date with Simone wasn't a total loss! These new faces will help me practice and tune-up my skills.' With all the practice and preparation for the cruise tournament, neither Danny, nor Christy ever mentioned anything about the cruise that they were unknowingly, both, going to be on. Neither one had an inkling. When they played, they kept their silence about anything personal. Over the next two months, their passionate feelings for each other only grew more. They both wanted to open up, but were going to wait until after the cruise.

Chapter 9
Christy Sharpens Her Skills

The *following week time seemed to be flying by for Christy. It was Thursday while having lunch with her girlfriends from work when she realized it and said, "Where is the time going. I guess I'm thinking so much about my vacation cruise that I lost all sense of time. I know I got a lot of work done, but I feel like October is going to get here and I'm not gonna be prepared for the tournament. Any suggestions?" Her friend Debra spoke up and said, "I have one. Why don't you get some people together and practice. I mean, under real conditions." Christy immediately said, "That's a great idea! I'm so excited about the cruise that I wasn't thinking. Let's see, who should I play against? I have to think about strategies and honing my skills. You know, it's not just a matter of who gets the best cards. It's more of a mind game that wins." Debra spoke up and said, "Yes, I know." Laughing out loud she continued, "I know who you can play against. How about Carl and Henry from HR, and...Tony from Accounting, and that nice looking dumb* *hunk Larry from Public Relations? Didn't you and Larry date at one time?"*

Thinking about Debra's choices for a moment, Christy laughed and said, "Debra that's brilliant! I see you understand the mental part of the game and I know where you're going with it. That's why you selected those guys didn't you?" Jeanette, one of the other ladies at the table said, "I'm not sure I would have selected them. Tell me why that's a great idea?" Debra laughed and said, "Think about it! Christy has to use ALL *the tools that she was blessed with when she's playing. I know how to play the game. Not as good as her, but I know that sometimes you have to psyche-out or distract your opponents. Winning is not just about the cards you're dealt. Sometimes you can confuse and sidetrack your opponents as well with...*other than cards. If you catch my drift."

Still not quite sure Jeanette asked, "Oh I think I get it. I'm not a poker player but I think I understand. But explain to me, why you chose these guys?" Debra went on, "Tony is unemotional. He's a numbers guy. He will help her sharpen her skills because he will be the biggest challenge for her since he'll be the hardest to read. Larry from PR will be easily distracted. Christy can practice using her sensuality to see what distracts guys like him. Whether it's licking her lips, or wearing a low cut blouse and reaching across the table to give him a cheap distracting thrill, thereby taking his mind off the game and confusing him. Carl and Henry are really nice guys, but as you know, they're gay, and these two can get very emotional very easily. Christy can use them to get sharper at reading their facial expressions, and body language, to figure out what kind of poker hands they have." Christy laughed and said, "Exactly! That's great. Besides, Carl and Henry are excellent cooks, and if this doesn't go well, at least I'll enjoy their food. And yes, I had one date with Larry the octopus! All hands and no brains!" The ladies laughed as each one raised a glass of iced tea to toast to Christy's success against the guys.

After lunch, they went back to the office. Christy wasted no time arranging a poker game with the unsuspecting four males for Saturday evening at Carl's apartment. She explained that she wanted to practice, and did not want to play any high stakes games, but to keep it friendly. They agreed to a fifty dollar limit on a nickel-dime game of Texas Hold 'em poker, with a maximum call of two dollars, and only allow 'All In' bets during the last hour of play. Rushing home later that day Christy sat down to dinner with Stacie and told her all about practicing poker with the guys. Stacie had a good laugh when her mom explained her strategy, and how it was Debra's brilliant idea. The rest of the week leading up to Saturday was business as usual and fairly uneventful.

Every night during the week without fail Christy and Danny met up to play together online. Their conversations were interesting, and deeper, and their bond was getting tighter even though they kept the intimate details of their identities concealed from each other. They liked that mysterious feeling of keeping their fantasy about each other intact.

Saturday night at about six p.m. Christy and they guys gathered at Carl's house. Everyone was on time and without fail Carl and Henry prepared some incredibly delicious gourmet snacks. They served them with a choice of wine or imported beer. They were great hosts and always made with funny wisecracking and witty humor. They even managed to get emotionless *Tony from Accounting to laugh several times. Larry remained fixated on Christy since she wore a low cut red blouse. When picking an outfit from her closet, she chose red, and laughed as she explained to her daughter, before leaving for Carl's place, that she wanted to* 'wave it in the bull's face' *like a Matador before the kill.*

Within about half an hour they began to play. She played masterfully. Several times Larry overplayed his hand because he was watching Christy's gestures which she made on purpose and stealthily directed them at Larry. She was able to read Carl's and Henry's faces and body language and outplayed them as well. Tony was the only one she really had a problem with as he beat her several times after she misread him. Larry was the first one to lose his entire fifty dollar position, and was eliminated. Christy took him out of the game with a full house winning hand over his club flush. When he lost, Larry became upset and left because, as he said, he "didn't like getting beat by a woman!" The players remained silent until Larry finished voicing his immature opinion and left the apartment.

The rest of them took a five minute break from the game and laughed at Larry's poor sportsmanship and childish behavior. Carl laughed and said, "I can imagine what he would have said if I beat him!" Christy responded, "He always was a sore loser. He thinks he knows how to play just because he's good looking. I like him as a co-worker but that's where it ends. I have a funny story about Larry. Listen. You'll laugh at this incident regarding Larry's intelligence. One night I was invited to play at our boss's house. Larry was there. It was dealer's choice which means, whoever's turn it was at dealing the cards, that person selected the game to be played. When Larry's turn at dealer came he selected Black Jack. Larry is in Public Relations and I think it's because he flunked math in every grade from high school through college. Well anyway he had a few beers so he was kinda woozy too. As he was dealing the cards he was miscounting everyone's hand at the table. When he finally got the card counting correct he dealt himself his cards.

He had five cards which added up to twenty one but he kept saying twenty. We all looked at him and waited. He put down the deck and kept looking at his cards, and saying twenty, right? Finally some guy at the table said, 'Hey man. You called the game and you can't even count! I suggest you take off your shoes and socks and unzip your fly. Between your fingers, toes, and anything else you find, maybe you'll be able to count to twenty one.' The whole table erupted in laughter. Larry got mad and got up and left. We had someone drive him home. After he left, we kept laughing as somebody kept calling Black Jack every time it was their turn as dealer. But before dealing that person took off their shoes, and said they would keep their pants on, and ask the rest of us if he made twenty one. That was too funny. And they never let him live it down at the office."

The four of them laughed as they continued with their game until ten o'clock, when they called it quits. Christy was the winner. They agreed to meet every other Saturday night, and play until she left for her cruise. After arriving home later that night, before going to bed, she had to play a few hands of poker online, using her phone app with her fantasy man Clint.

Every other Saturday, like clockwork, the five of them got together to play. They decided to drop the maximum amount of play to thirty dollars. Larry stepped up his game, but he was still paying more attention to

Christy's sexual appeal, and her choice of clothes that accentuated her beautiful body, than the game at hand. The next time it was Tony who won the match. She had the other players pegged. Tony faked out Christy during several hands. She made it a point to focus on his play. She made mental notes tying Tony's gestures to the hands he held that beat her. After a couple more Saturday games she figured him out. But more importantly she learned to read more subtle signs coming from someone with a great poker face. Feeling better armed, and stepping up her play, she felt her skills improved to the point where she was more confident in her abilities.

One night during a dinner that Stacie prepared, Christy spoke about her excitement for the trip and her preparedness for the tournament. As they spoke Stacie asked, "By the way mom. I meant to ask but kept forgetting. What about this guy Clint that you play with online every night? Did you two talk about this cruise, and if so, is he gonna be there too? Are you finally gonna meet him?" Her mom answered, "No. No meetings at this point. We don't even know who each other is yet. And we want to keep it that way for a while. I have not mentioned anything about this cruise. That is NOT the place I want to have our first meeting." Laughing, Christy continued, "If we met on the ship and it did NOT go well, then where do you think I could go? I certainly can't just up and leave. I would have to jump ship! Hahaha!" Stacie laughed and replied, "Don't worry mom. We're both black belts. Between the both of us we should be able to handle this guy." Christy said, "Another thing I considered is that there will most likely be a lot of men on board. What happens if I meet Mr. Right, and Clint turns out to be Mr. Wrong? Besides, I don't want to have any distractions of a meeting with Clint while I'm playing in a tournament. Don't want to take a chance on ruining my focus on the game. I'm excited about that. Also, we're going together, and I want to spend some time with you. God knows we've been going in different directions and we haven't had any quality mother-daughter time for a long while! I miss that, and I want to make up for some of that lost time." Stacie said, "Me too mom. But what happens to our time together if you meet Mr. Right? Hahaha!" Stacie and her mom laughed when Christy responded, "We'll see. If that happens I only hope Mr. Right's first name doesn't turn out to be, 'Always'"!

Later that night just before Christy fell asleep she whispered as she closed her eyes, "I can't wait to meet Clint. How I wish I knew who he is?" She drifted off to sleep and had a dream. In her dream she's sitting up in bed. It's a large bedroom. The walls, ceiling, and floor are bright white. In front of her is a long curtain that reaches to the floor. To the right of her stand Henry dressed in red and Carl dressed in green outfits. She's

confused as she looks at them. She then spoke to them
and their conversation went like this:

CHRISTY: (confused expression) Carl? Henry? What's
going on here?

CARL: (purses his lips-smiles) We're your fairy god-
brothers and we're here to grant your wish.

CHRISTY: (puzzled look) What wish?

HENRY: (snickers at Carl-then at Christy) Just before
you fell asleep you wished to know who Clint is.

CARL: (snickers) We see you playing that game and we
know how you feel about Clint. Just tell us you want to
see him and we'll roll up that curtain and you'll meet him.

CHRISTY: (anxious-swallows) Yes. I want to meet him.

Carl and Henry both make a rolling motion with
their index finger on their right hand and the curtain
slowly rises. Initially Christy squints with some disgust as
bare feet are revealed. Slowly going higher she's
surprised when she sees a pants crotch with the zipper
undone. Christy is in disbelief at what she sees as the
curtain rolls up higher and a pair of hands scramble to
zip up the pants. Continuing faster the curtain revealed
the person. It's Larry with a very puzzled expression as he
looks in and around the room. Christy looks at Carl and
Henry who are gazing lustfully at Larry.

CHRISTY: *(Mouth halfway open. With a fearful look she shakes her head)* **That can't be Clint?**

HENRY: *(winks at Christy-giggles) Oh no girlfriend! He's ours. We gonna keep him and play Black Jack. (Henry and Carl look at each other-silly giggle and high five as Larry stands next to them)*

CARL: *(winks at Christy-laughs) And we're gonna make sure he counts to twenty one every time!*

CHRISTY: *(sighs expresses relief-serious tone)* **You can have him! Now please show me Clint**!

Carl and Henry roll down the curtain, then they make the rolling motion with their index finger on their right hand and the curtain slowly rises. Christy's expression changed to a smile as the curtain rolled up faster and revealed a well dressed man in a dark suit.

As the curtain rolls up to his neck area and just about to reveal his face Christy is awaken by the ringing of her phone. She opens her eyes and leaning forward she has a disappointed expression. She picks up her phone and looks at it. Then she smiles and answers her phone as she brushes her hair with her hand, "Stacie your timing is **awful**. *(pause) I'm excited too. (pause) We're packed and ready to leave tomorrow. (pause) Okay. I'll meet you there in an hour."*

Chapter 10
Danny's Home Tournaments

With *help from two of his friends, setting up the house for a twenty-player tournament took about three hours that Saturday. There was ample parking around his neighborhood, and the neighbors never complained because they all threw parties, and used the same areas for their guests to park. Carpooling by the players made this a non-issue anyway as there were never more than five cars used to transport everyone and Danny's driveway accommodated three of them. The first Saturday night game was a warm up for him. Everyone arrived at least an hour early in order to meet and get to know the new people. The group consisted of twelve men, and eight women. All of whom considered themselves excellent poker players. The rules for refreshments were to bring your own beverage and snacks. But no hard liquor was allowed for various reasons. Mainly to keep the game civil and not lose control by anyone's over indulgence in strong alcohol.*

Before starting, everyone anteed-up their fifty dollars into the house pot and received five hundred dollars in poker chips. There were five tables consisting of four players at each table. To avoid players from sitting next to people they knew, table assignment was done by drawing a card from a deck that only contained aces through fives. This took some people out of their comfort zone by arranging the seating via a random draw. The players were excited as play started. There was a two hour limit of initial play with 'All In' calls suspended until the last fifteen minutes of play. At the end of two hours, the top player from each table earned a seat at the final table, and was 'in the money.' In the event of a tie, they played an All In, final open hand, winner-moves-on game. The final game was to be played with no time limit and no betting limits. Of the one thousand dollar house pot the; first place winner received three hundred fifty dollars; second place player received two hundred fifty dollars; third place player received two hundred dollars; fourth and fifth place players each received one hundred dollars.

When play began, Danny was seated at table number four with two other men and one woman. He knew one player well. The other two were his challenges. Not taking anyone lightly, he played his game, and played it at the top of his skill level. He handily won the first two games, folded early with lousy cards on the second hand, then won the next three. They were nearing the two hour limit and Danny's table had already eliminated two players.

It was now down to him and a woman named Vivian. She tried her best to distract him with her body language and sexual appeal but he never fell for that strategy. Thinking about what she was trying to do he then pretended he was distracted as he watched her every move including her breathing. When he noticed her nervously gulp some air and flinch her left eye he knew she was bluffing. Just like she did in an earlier hand when he was watching her, after he folded, as she bluffed her way to a win during a showdown with another player.

He surprised her when he called, "All In!" and won the pot with a pair of eights to her Ace King high card hand. Danny was congratulated by the players at his table as he waited for the others to complete their matches before taking a seat at the final table. As they waited one of the new people asked him where he learned to play so well. Danny laughed at first and told him that it was his first time playing and that he marked the cards on every deck before they started. They laughed because they knew better since all the decks were brand new and the seals were never broken open until the games began. Then Danny explained his poker playing background and about the tournament on his upcoming cruise.

After table two's sudden death match ended in exciting fashion where one player drew a higher card flush of the same suit, the five finalists consisting of two women and three men took their seats at the championship table. Danny knew one of the men but the others were new to him. He thought, 'Good. At least these new ones will make me work.' He was pleased by the matches since it was exactly what he expected to encounter on the cruise. Which was of course, all new people.

When final play began, Danny's strategy was, unless he had incredible hole cards, such as a high pair or high suited cards, that he was going to fold so that he could observe the competition. He folded the first two hands, which were horrible, and watched the other players, to pick up on their idiosyncrasies. He spotted several on each new player whether it was breathing heavy from excitement or shallow when they tried to bluff, or nervous blinking. He then experimented with the third hand.

After three people folded it left Danny playing against one of the women. He studied her movements and recognized something she did before when he picked up on her insecurity with her play. She pulled on her earlobe twice. Sensing she had a mediocre hand he acted like he was insecure with his hand by hesitating. She was faked out by his act and called, "All In!" Danny's expression never changed when he waited a few seconds before saying, "Call!," and pushed his chips into the pot.

She had a devilish smile on her face, thinking she beat him, when she turned over her hole cards and said, "Two pairs. Aces and Tens!" Expressionless, he stared at her before turning over his hole cards and said, "Three Fours!" Her face went from smiling to confused as her jaw dropped and her eyes squinted. She said, "I could have sworn I had you beat! You had that look on your face like you were bluffing! Damn, you're good!" That made Danny smile as he said, "You're good too. I almost folded. I appreciate the compliment." Turning back to the game he thought, 'One down. three to go.'

Focusing on the players at the table the next few hands were easy wins for Danny. After two more players were eliminated it was down to him and a new guy he just met that evening. In a twist of play, the man decided to call, "All In!", and play the entire hand blind, which means that he was not going to look at his hole cards. Danny thought, 'We have a shit poker player here. Ok. Now how should I handle this clown? Maybe I underestimated him!' Since this guy never looked at his hole cards there was no use trying to decipher his expressions.

Danny waited to see his hole cards before he made his next move. He was too smart at this game and *not about to bet it all on lousy hole cards. Danny had three times the amount of chips his opponent had and it helped that his hole cards were a pair of Queens. It was a no brainer as he decided to 'Call' the bet but not to reveal any hole cards until all the community cards were dealt. The dealer laid down the five community cards. They were; Ace, Three, Five, Queen, Queen. His opponent went first since he was called and turned over his hole cards. The first was an Ace that brought a smile to Danny's opponent. Then turning over the second card his opponent said, "Yes!" The second card was also an Ace. Smiling and believing he won the pot he looked at Danny and his big smile was immediately wiped off his face when Danny turned over his two Queens.*

Stunned, his opponent asked him, "How did you do that?" Danny responded, "I cheated." There were about fourteen people who remained and they all busted out in laughter at Danny's response. Taking first place everyone congratulated Danny on his win. The house pot was distributed to the five finalists according to their placement. After about another hour of talking, and before they all left Danny's house, they agreed this was the way they wanted to play future matches. A couple of people stayed behind for about half an hour to help him clean up. He thanked them for their help as they left. He was tired and ready for bed but he fought his sleepiness long enough to meet up with Pretty Cowgirl, play a few hands, and chat with her before going to sleep.

As usual Sunday was family get together day and everyone gathered at Danny's house. No matter how much of a routine it was he savored every moment with his children, in-laws, and especially his grandkids. As usual, they drank, told jokes, laughed, and ate dinner. They were anxious to hear about the match that went on the night before and he was only too happy to fill them in on the events. Chris and Stephen were excited about it and asked if they could play in future games. Danny joked and everyone laughed when he said, "You guys? Sure I'll be glad to take your money. Why don't you save the embarrassment of losing to me and just throw your money out the window when you drive past my house?" The conversation then went to Danny's playing online with his fantasy partner.

Chris asked, "Hey dad. How's it going with your mystery woman and your online poker playing? What's her name again? Pretty Lady?" Danny smiled and answered, "Her name is Pretty Cowgirl and everything is going fine. So far our relationship is platonic and, to date, we've kept our identities a secret. So I don't know who she is and she doesn't know who I am." Stephen asked, "Do you ever see it going any further and revealing your identities?" Danny answered, "Yes we both do. But we're waiting for a while. It's nice to have a little fantasy in our lives so we're keeping it that way for now." Vicky then asked, "Did you talk about the cruise and the tournament with her and do you think she would be interested?" Danny shook his head and said, "No way. I don't want to talk about anything like that. Being a captive audience on a ship is NOT some place I want to make my first meeting with anyone. For obvious reasons. Besides I want to focus on fun, and the match, and spend some quality time with my daughter."

Noticing a funny expression on Donna's face he asked, "Honey, is there something you want to ask me?" She blushed and said, "Well yeah. I was just wondering how you two are getting along. I mean I heard a lot about long distance relationships and ones where people know the other person's identity, but where they never met in person. I heard about some of those where the people fell for each other or developed strong emotional feelings for one another. Is any of that happening between you too? (Laughing) Or is it some kind of cyber poker sex you're having? Hahaha!"

Danny laughed and said, "You might have something there. I never thought of it like that. Just kidding. You know Donna? In a way we have *developed some feelings for each other. It's weird and neither one of us can explain it. But we're being patient. I've decided that I'm going to open up to her after I get back from the cruise. I don't want anything spoiling this and throwing me off my game. We already have some idea about each other since we talked a lot about deep subjects and share quite a bit of common ground in our beliefs about life. Also, about things like working out, and staying in great shape. We're both single. At least that's what she told me, and from what I can gather, I don't see her having any reason to lie. If she turns out to be what I imagine she is, then,* **I'll marry her!**" *Everyone at the table was quiet as they were stunned by Danny's 'marry her' comment. Seeing their reaction he laughed and said, "Remember I said,* **IF** *she turns out to be what I imagine she is, so don't think I'm jumping the gun here people!"*

The subject turned to the upcoming cruise and the shore excursions Vicky and her father planned. With excitement in her voice Vicky said, "Dad arranged and prepaid several other things we're gonna do together. One of them is horseback riding on the beach, another is swimming with the dolphins, and the third is parasailing. I wanted to do these things since I was a child, and I can't wait." Danny was always delighted seeing either of his kids so excited to do something with him.

He looked at Stephen and said, "Don't worry about her! I had to work on toughening her up when she was younger. She was too scared to do a lot of these things when she was a child. It wasn't until she was a teenager that I was able to convince her to ride the roller coasters at the amusement park. After that I couldn't keep her off of any wild rides. One year I took my family with me on my business trip to Ohio. The amusement park there has a couple of huge wooden roller coasters. One of them has a loop on it. All made of wood. This thing jerked us around so hard and fast that I found it difficult to ride, and I'm a roller coaster fanatic. Anyway, when we got off the damned thing, I felt like my neck was dislocated because we were jerked around so much. Vicky and Chris jumped out and ran to the front of the line to get back on board. They tried to get us to ride again, but Rachel and I backed out. We bought a couple of cherry snow cones and watched them go three more times, and cringed every time we saw that thing go around the loop! I guess that boosted her courage enough to get married later on since I once told her that marriage is like a roller coaster. I bet you she would be first in line to swim with the sharks if they had that event on this cruise!" Vicky smiled at him and said, "Why not, dad? But I would probably only do that once!" Everyone at the table laughed at Vicky's witty comeback.

The rest of the evening with the family was fun yet uneventful. Cleaning the table, washing the dishes, having a few drinks, and conversation. After everyone went home, he secured the house, then went upstairs, showered, and got into bed. Accessing his cell phone he opened his online poker app, found his Pretty Cowgirl playing, and joined her for almost an hour. Play was still very even between them and the conversation was always pleasurable. After exiting the app and returning his phone to its charging cradle, Danny laid in bed and day dreamed about him and Pretty Cowgirl for a while before falling asleep.

After falling asleep Danny dreams about meeting Pretty Cowgirl. In his dream he is sitting up in bed. The walls, ceiling, and floor are bright white. In front of him is a curtain reaching all the way to the floor. Suddenly two figures appear and flank the curtain. On the left is Simone and on the right is Cathy. Both dressed in long gowns and adorned in jewelry. To the right is Cathy's boyfriend videotaping them dressed in a curtain wrapped around him like a toga. With a confused expression Danny talks to them. Their conversation and the events in his dream went like this:

DANNY: (squints his eyes at Cathy & Simone) Where am I and what are all of you doing here?

SIMONE: (smiles) We're your fairy god-sisters and we heard your wish. You want to meet Pretty Cowgirl, don't you?

DANNY: (still confused and apprehensive) Yes. But.....

CATHY: (interrupts and smiles) But nothing. We're here to grant you your wish! Tell us when you're ready and we'll bring her to you.

DANNY: (shrugs his shoulders and smiles) Yes. Please go ahead.

Simone and Cathy pull on the curtain string. As the curtain begins to rise up from the floor they heard a commotion from behind the curtain. With concerned expressions Simone and Cathy pull the curtain strings quicker. As the curtain was rising Danny saw several people pushing and shoving. The fully opened curtain revealed Peggy and her parents. Danny was stunned. Cathy & Simone were angry!

SIMONE: (yelling at them) **Stop it Peggy! Get out and take your creepy parents with you! And tell Pretty Cowgirl to come here on your way out!**

They drop the curtain down and nod at each other.

CATHY: (peeks behind the curtain-smiles-nods) Danny? Get ready to meet your Pretty Cowgirl!

Simone and Cathy pull the string and the curtain began to rise slowly revealing a beautiful pair of legs. Up further it showed a lovely dress and hands folded in front of her stomach. Further up revealed a beautiful figure.

Just as the curtain reached her neck the sound of Danny's phone alarm woke him up. He quickly rose to a sitting up position and looked around the room trying to gain his perspective. Realizing that it was only dream he was nonetheless very disappointed. Shaking his head with frustration he holds up his phone and before answering it he said out loud, **"Great timing!"**

The next few weeks were fairly smooth and routine. Danny played well in the next two poker tournaments, winning one and coming in second in the other. He was ready for the cruise and all set to go, and so was Vicky. He never looked back at the dating site and put all those incidents behind him. He focused on his vacation as well as after his vacation where he anxiously awaited finding out the true identity of Pretty Cowgirl.

Chapter 11
All Aboard!

October *29th was upon them. Vicky's and Danny's flight arrived in Miami, Florida in plenty of time for them to catch a short cab ride to the ship's terminal and board the ocean liner. There were no problems with checking their luggage and going through security. All their paperwork was in order and they were given the green light to board. After boarding the ship, like all passengers, they went to one of the decks where lunch was being served and waited there until they were advised, by the Cruise Director, that their rooms were ready. Danny told Vicky to go to the Lido Deck, get a table, and he would join her there for lunch as soon as he cleared some issues with the ship's Client Services. By the time she got there, all the tables were taken. Looking around Vicky spotted a table for four that was occupied by two women. Asking if she could join them, they graciously said "Yes, of course." She sat down and waited for her dad.*

It took Danny almost half an hour with Client Services to ensure he and his daughter were registered for the shore excursions that he paid for in advance. While waiting for her dad, Vicky conversed with the two women at the table. "Thanks for letting me join you. My name is Vicky Fenton. I'm from Charlotte, North Carolina." The younger woman spoke up, and returning her greeting she said, "Hi Vicky. It's nice to meet you, and you're very welcome. My name is Stacie Darren, and this beautiful woman is my older sister (laughing). I'm just kidding. This is my beautiful mom, Christy Darren, and we're from Orlando, Florida. Who are you here with?" Vicky smiled and answered, "That's funny. You're here with your mom and I'm here with my dad. He's here for the poker tournament and asked me to come along. I loved what I read about the cruise and my husband was fine with me coming and him staying home with our son. We have separate rooms and this is also a chance to have some quality 'father and daughter' time together. He should be here any minute. He went to check on our shore excursions. I'm really excited. How about you two? Anyone else joining you?"

Christy smiled as she listened to Vicky and answered, "Nope. It's the same thing with us. We're here to spend some quality 'mother and daughter' time together. And I am also here for the poker tournament. So when your dad gets here I'll get to meet one of my *challengers. Am I right if I assume your mom does not play poker?" Vicky answered, "Actually it was my mom who taught my dad how to play. Unfortunately my mom passed away a few years ago." Christy's smile quickly faded, and reaching over she patted Vicky's hand and said, "Oh please forgive me. I'm terribly sorry." Vicky smiled and said, "That's Ok, and thanks. She was great, and for however long we had her, I cherish that time." With a compassionate look Christy replied, "That's great that you see it and feel it that way. As for me, it was my husband who taught me how to play poker. And coincidentally, he passed away years ago as well. Stacie and I feel the same way about my husband John that you do about your mom." Vicky shook her head and said, "I'm sorry about your loss as well. Looks like we've got a lot in common already." Looking at Christy now Vicky thought, 'What a beauty! Dad's gonna flip when he sees her! She'll probably do the same when she sees him. God I hope he gets here before they leave! I need to stall them.'*

Trying to buy some time for her dad to get there, and keeping the conversation going, Vicky said, "Changing the subject, what do you two do for a living?" Christy answered, "I'm a Regional Director for a major Pharmaceutical company." Stacie chimed in, "And I'm a Registered Nurse with Orlando Hospital System. How about you and your dad?" Vicky answered, "My dad is a Vice President with a major national bank. As for me, I too am an R.N. I'm the Assistant Director of Nursing at Charlotte Medical System." The two younger women smiled at each other seeing how they had so much more in common. Looking around Vicky spotted her father standing near the pool looking for her. Standing up she waved and called out to him. Seeing Danny waving back and starting to walk towards them Stacie thought, 'Oh my God. What a good looking guy. My mom is gonna flip when she sees him!' Looking up at Danny, Christy did a double take as she thought, 'Wow. What a handsome man. Hope he's not anything like Larry!'

Using his best poker face he could not help but stare at Christy as he walked to the table. He thought, 'Lucky for me that Vicky chose that table. What a goddess! Please God, don't let her be anything like Peggy, or Cathy, or (shuttering inside) BobSimone!' Reaching the table he said, "Well hello everyone! Vicky? Would you please introduce me to these lovely ladies?" Vicky introduced them saying, "This is Stacie and her older sister Christy Darren. Stacie and Christy. Meet my older brother Danny." Catching on quickly he said, "Very nice to meet you." Chuckling he continued, "Well I guess my little sister told you about us."

Christy stood up, put on her best smile, reached over, shook Danny's hand and said, "Very nice to meet you. And yes, we had a very good conversation with her. You have a very charming daughter. She told us you've entered the poker tournament. That's what I'm here for as well. This is my daughter's birthday present to me." Both sat down, then Danny said, "How thoughtful! That's a great present. This is the first time I've played in a large tournament in a long time. I used to play once a year or so up until a few years ago." Christy cut in and said, "Vicky told us. So sorry about your wife. This is my first one in a long while too. You see I also lost my spouse years ago...Well? Are you ready for the challenge?" Danny smiled and said, "Absolutely! How about you?" Christy said, "Same here!"

While they were talking and only focused on each other Vicky made eye contact with Stacie. They both smiled seeing the expressions on their parents' faces who were totally oblivious to the rest of the world as they held a conversation. Vicky and Stacie shook their heads and winked at each other. The wheels in their heads were turning and they had the same thought in their minds: 'How could they help pair these two up?'

Breaking up the conversation was the sound of the cruse ship's whistle signaling to get the passengers' attention. The Cruise Director came over the loud speaker announcing all the passengers' luggage was delivered to the rooms and for the passengers to now make their way to their rooms to confirm receipt of all of their belongings. Danny, Christy, Stacie, and Vicky stood up and thanked each other for the good company. As they *started to walk to the Lido Deck exit doors they looked at their room numbers and noticed they were ten rooms apart on the same deck. They proceeded to walk together two by two and continued their conversation down one flight of stairs to the Promenade Deck.*

Danny and Christy hit it off well and agreed to meet later that night for dinner with their daughters. Vicky and Stacie walked behind them and, like new best friends, they snickered and whispered to each other. Stacie said, "Did you see the way they looked at each other when they first saw each other? My mom did a double take. I've never seen her do that before. Hahaha!" Vicky snickered and whispered, "I know my dad and I saw that look in his eyes when he first saw your mom and while he was talking to her. Also, it's a great thing that they both love poker. Stacie? Are you thinking what I'm thinking?" Stacie answered, "I believe I do." Vicky asked, "Do you wanna play matchmaker? Hahaha!" Stacie said, "That's what I'm thinking. Oh yeah! Let's do it. I like you and I like your dad. He's really handsome and seems to be a very nice guy. If he's genuine...look out Danny!" Vicky answered, "Same here. I really like you and your mom. She's gorgeous and smart. And if your mom is genuine...look out Christy!" They both chuckled and high fived each other. The young ladies exchanged room numbers so they could meet later on to plan their matchmaking strategy.

Reaching their rooms first, Danny and Vicky told Christy and Stacie good bye for now, and they would see them later for dinner. Danny helped Vicky carry her luggage into her room before checking into his room. While in her room, she took the opportunity to ask her dad what he thought about Christy. She asked, "So dad. What do you think about the lady you just met?" He looked at her, sighed and said, "She really turned my head at first sight. She's gorgeous and smart too. She can hold a conversation and challenge you. I would like to get to know more about her. I'm also gonna rely on you since you seemed to hit if off well with her daughter. By the way, what were you two schoolgirls talking and giggling about anyway?"

Not realizing he noticed her and Stacie's reaction caught her off guard. She knew her dad was very observant, but sold him short thinking his total focus was on Christy. She thought quickly and said, "We have a lot in common with each other. We're both R.N.'s. We're both here with our widowed parent to spend some quality time together. Both of you are in the poker tournament. And we were giggling at how you two were locked and loaded in conversation, and the silly looks you both had when you first saw each other. We thought it was funny." Danny smiled and said, "I can see that. But in the meanwhile I want to keep my promise and spend some quality time with you. I don't know when we'll get this kind of opportunity again." Vicky smiled back and said, "We spend a lot of quality time every Sunday too. So if this beautiful lady and you hit it off, then I say, go for it! You never know when you may get this kind of opportunity again either!" He smiled and gave his daughter a hug. Then he left for his room so he could unpack his luggage. After he left, Vicky's thoughts were of her dad and Christy. She thought, 'I hope Christy is as genuine as her beauty. I don't want her to be some phony and hurt my dad bad enough to make him give up on finding a partner altogether. I only have seven days to make this work. Otherwise he's gonna be spending his nights at home alone, and playing poker with some bimbo named Pretty Cowgirl. Whenever I've seen women give themselves pseudo names to prop themselves up they usually turn out to be the opposite of it. I need to get a hold of Stacie as soon as possible.'

Opening the door and entering their room Christy and Stacie brought in their luggage and sat their suitcases on their beds. While unpacking and putting away their clothes, bathroom, and personal items Christy noticed that Stacie kept a big smile on her face. She asked, "Ok young lady. What's with that big smile pasted on your face since we left the Lido Deck?" Stacie answered, "I think I just made a new best friend mom. And to go along with my new BF is a really handsome dude of a dad. First time I ever saw you do a double take *when you first met a nice looking guy. What do you think of him mom?" Christy answered, "He sure is a handsome man. And very smart. The only time I ever remember doing a double take is when I first met your father. Well, to tell you the truth, I would like to try to get to know Danny. But first things first. We came here to spend some very important mother and daughter time together. You're important to me honey. We've been through a lot since your dad passed away, and I want to be sure I make some good memories with you. You understand, don't you?" Stacie answered, "Sure I do mom. But remember that we see each other almost every day and if you hit it off with this guy, then I say,* go for it! *We live right around the corner from several cruise ship ports. It won't be hard to go on another one together. Don't worry about me. I'll be just fine mom." After a smile, and a hug they resumed unpacking and organizing their belongings for their seven day voyage. Watching her mom, Stacie thought, 'I want to see her happy so she can get on with her life, and quit staying home nights playing that stupid game on her phone with that Clint guy. Gotta work fast with Vicky. We only have seven days. Boy oh boy, I hope Danny is the real deal.'*

While Vicky was relaxing after unpacking her belongings, there was a knock on her door. Getting up she opened the door and smiled. She said, "I was just thinking about you. C'mon in and sit down." Closing the door she said, "Glad you showed up Stacie. We gotta talk and I think you're here for the same concerns as I have." Stacie smiled and said, "If it's because we want to get our parents together and only have seven days? Then you're right!" They both laughed when Vicky answered, "That's exactly what I was worried about! This is gonna take some serious planning and manipulation on both our parts. You think we can pull it off? I mean my dad is NOT a fast worker. He likes to take relationships really really slow!" Stacie answered, "Looks like they have even more in common every time we talk about something. Mom is the same way. I never saw her rush into anything with a guy. She usually meets such jerks who only want to jump into bed as soon as she says hello." Vicky said, "Yep. Every time you or I say something, we chalk up another item they have in common. Dad had some miserable luck with women who turned out to be...well let's just say anything but the right one. The trouble is that it appears we're dealing with two sloths here when it comes time to relationships. Although, my dad is probably the last of the romantic gentlemen."

Stacie stood up and said, "That's a good thing. It's what mom loved so much about my dad. We may be able to pull this off." Vicky asked, "Hey Stacie. Do you and your mom have any shore excursions planned?" Stacie answered, "No. We were going to just wing it when we got here. Why? What are you thinking?" Vicky answered, "We've got three events planned. I think we can get them together on at least one of them. Do you think you can talk your mom into doing one with her? There aren't many people signed up for them, so we should be able to keep them close to each other during two of them. I mean, I can fake an injury and suggest he use my ticket to take your mom. There are no refunds, and it's on a use it or lose it basis. What do you say?" Stacie thought a moment and answered, "Let's let that one be a last resort. Mom doesn't like to take things, especially something as expensive as an excursion from someone she doesn't know. Sorry to say this, but especially from a man she just met. She never wants to feel obligated in any way. But if we see that they are hitting it off early and are spending time together, then I think she might be ok with that. We've got to get pretty busy though. Seven days are going to fly by quickly. I better get back to mom before she starts wondering where I went off to. I told her I'd be back in ten minutes. I'm All In if you are." Both laughing at Stacie's use of the poker term as Vicky said, "I Call you! All in!" Standing up to leave they shook hands, winked, and hugged before Stacie left the room.

Chapter 12
Day 1 - Cruising In Style

Dinner *in the main dining room was considered an upscale, and on certain occasions, an elegant, affair that required more formal attire. It was expected for all guests to dress, at minimum, in neat, resort-casual appropriate clothing. Danny only owned classy clothing and showed up in a custom tailored grey suit and tie while Vicky wore a lovely long pink dress. They waited at the main entrance for their company. Christy and Stacie arrived about five minutes later. Seeing Christy enter the room wearing an elegant red evening gown took Danny's breath away. When she saw him dressed in his handsome suit she did another double take and began to feel as nervous as a school girl on her first date that just happen to be prom night. Danny felt a little awkward since there were no florists onboard, and could not perform his practice of presenting each lady with a red rose. Escorted by the Maitre d' to their table Danny extended his arm to Christy. She smiled and* *nodded as she hooked his arm and proceeded to their table. For the first time in a long time Danny actually was weak kneed as he walked with this beauty. He kept thinking, 'I sure hope this night lasts a long time.' Christy felt her face flush as she thought, 'I haven't felt like this in a long time.' Their daughters walked behind them arm in arm as they mimicked them and snickered. They even managed to sneak in a high five.*

Waiting until the ladies were seated Danny then took his place at the table. He started the conversation by complimenting the women on their excellent taste in dress and on their beauty. He said, "I'm very flattered to have such beautiful company. Thank you both for joining us for dinner." Turning to Stacie he said, "Forgive me for not taking the time earlier to speak with you Stacie. The conversation with your mom was so interesting that I lost track of time before we got a chance to talk earlier today. Tell me about yourself." Stacie looked at Vicky then turned to Danny and said, "That's OK. Well where do I start? I was born and raised in Florida. My dad taught me how to fish, play softball, and all sorts of other sports. He was concerned about me being able to defend myself so when I was five years old he enrolled me, and mom, in Martial Arts. We're still in the program and as of today we hold the rank of Second Degree Black Belts. Mom and I both hold Florida state titles in full contact competitions." Danny looked at Christy and smiled. Then they all laughed when he said, "Wow! That's great! I'm glad you warned me. But I feel safer now too!"

Stacie laughed as she continued, "Yes sir. My mom is dangerous and her hands are considered lethal weapons. Anyway, I graduated from a college in Orlando so I could be at home with mom and I still live at home. I really enjoy my work as a nurse. It's very rewarding." Danny asked her, "So I assume you're not married." Stacie answered, "Right. I'm taking my time and looking right now. No one serious in my life yet. I'm not too crazy about the men I've met. I haven't met anyone who really takes anything serious. They all want to have fun as they put it. Many of them have some bad habits that I'm not willing to overlook." Vicky spoke up saying, "Yeah. I know what you mean. I got lucky and found a keeper early on. I see what my friends are going through and I couldn't be more thankful." Danny turned to Vicky and winked before turning to Stacie and saying, "You're doing the right thing. Stick to your standards and don't drop them for anyone. Everyone deserves good things and good people in life. Glad to see you're not settling for anything less. You seem to have a good heart, and you certainly are beautiful, and I know it can be frustrating but I believe you'll eventually find happiness."

They had an enjoyable conversation all through dinner. Each one opened up and spoke about their background and especially about their family. They got to know a lot more about each other.

During the conversation Stacie stopped and laughed as she said, "It didn't dawn on me until just now Mr. Canton that you are the youngest and most handsome grandfather I've ever seen." Christy laughed and said, "Looking at you I have a hard time fathoming that myself." They laughed when he said, "Well I know I don't look it but I'm actually seventy two years old. (chuckling) And I owe it all to my children. Joking aside, the fact is that I became a father of twins at age eighteen. In fact that made my mom and dad grandparents at a younger age than me. Thank goodness though my kids were kind enough to wait for me to get into my forties before making me a grandfather. At first I felt really old when they said you're gonna be a grandpa! Ouch! But I love my kids and I missed the fun times we had during their childhood. So they gave me a second round. Now, I can't get enough of them. All my attention goes to the grandkids. (turning sarcastic) That's why I'm on this cruise. So I can give some much needed undivided time to my attention starved baby girl. Right honey?" Vicky laughed and answered, "Right, dear 'ole dad!" Danny turned to Stacie and snickering he said, "Oh by the way. Please call me Danny. Mr. Canton sounds so old."

Even though she was quiet, Christy was mainly observing and learning a lot about Danny's personality.

Not only so much from what he said but how he interacted uniquely and genuinely with her daughter. She also did the same with his daughter. She kept her guard up, and after studying him, she concluded that she very much liked what she saw. She knew Stacie was already sold on him from an earlier conversation they had in their ship's stateroom, and saw her daughter light up during her conversation with him during dinner. Listening to his daughter and hearing about their family gatherings during the weekends, as well as hearing about his son Chris the engineer and his Architect wife Donna spoke volumes about the quality of his character, and gave her a lot of insight about the kind of man Danny is. Christy thought, 'Holy Jeez! This is a second time it's happened to me in the last few months. It's so unusual for me to start having feelings about someone I just met and hardly know much about. First Clint...and now Danny. What's going on with me? I need to take a step back to make sure I'm not doing this out of desperation. That wouldn't be fair to me or anyone. Especially not fair to my daughter. I better skip the dancing tonight and just go to my room and try to sort this out. Yeah. I'm tired from the long drive today so I'll use that as an excuse.'

Even though he was involved in the majority of the conversations at the table, Danny was also very stealthily perceptive. Between the negotiating and people skills that he learned and used so well at all levels of business, board room meetings, and group discussions, he picked up on the way Christy quietly observed and gauged him and his daughter. Looking at Christy he said, "You're suddenly very quiet. Is everything OK?" She knew he caught on and seized the moment to make her excuse. She also used this as a test. She said, "Well after a long week at work and a long drive to Miami from Orlando, I believe it all caught up with me and now I'm just feeling pretty tired. I know it's early but I think I'll call it a night for me. I could use some downtime. I apologize if I ruined anyone's plans." Hearing this took Stacie and Vicky by complete surprise. They looked at each other with concern that perhaps something about Danny turned her off but neither one said a word.

Danny was taken by surprise and very disappointed but he covered it well. He threw Christy off when he responded, "I completely understand. I was looking forward to dancing and spending some more time together but I guess, if you're still interested, that can wait. I think I'll take a tour of the ship to get familiarized with where everything is before calling it a night myself. Vicky? Care to join your dear 'ole dad?"

Hiding her disappointment Vicky turned to him and said, "That's OK dad. I know you grandpa types can't take staying out too late. But Stacie and I are going to check out the club and piano bar." They laughed at her comment. Danny said, "OK. Wise guy. Just remember that when you get to my age." Christy snickered and again surprised him when she asked, "Danny? How about escorting Stacie's dear 'ole mom back to her cabin." Stacie's and Vicky's disappointment diminished when they heard Christy ask Danny for a private escort to her cabin. They did not realize it was going to be a test of his character. Little did Christy know it was also going to be a test of her character as well.

Standing up and excusing themselves from the others, Christy walked with Danny out of the dining room. Vicky looked at Stacie and said, "Well that was unnerving for a few moments. What do we do now? Any ideas?" Irritated and nervous Stacie replied, "You bet that was. My mom got me all uptight and pretty upset for a few moments. I thought I was gonna have to take her aside and have a private discussion with her about retiring early and leaving your dad high and dry. I'm worried that he might wander off and find someone else. Then, she asks him to walk her back to our room! I hope there's a Do Not Disturb sign hanging on the door knob when I get back. I may have to bunk with you if you don't mind." Vicky laughed and said, "You don't have to worry about that. My dad won't rush the physical part yet. They may kiss and get a little personal but he won't let it go too far and I don't think your mom will either. I think it may be part tired, and probably part test. What do you think?" Stacie replied, "I hope you're right, and if so, then I hope *my mom also gets tested. Ok. Well? What do you say we go check out the clubs and see what's going on there? When I get back with my mom, I'm gonna find out why she did this and get back with you. Then maybe we can come up with some ideas and we can go to work on them tomorrow." They agreed and getting up from the table they left together to check out the ship's night life.*

As Christy and Danny passed by one of the stores next to the piano bar room they stopped to see the items in the store window. It was a jewelry store that offered luxurious duty free items. As she took a couple of steps away from Danny a drunk man in his late twenty's bumped into her almost knocking her over. Danny quickly walked up behind her to make sure she was alright. She said, "Hey mister. Watch where you're going!" The young man turned to her and said, "Hey pretty lady. I'm so sorry. Wow! You're beautiful. How about coming back to my cabin and forgiving me?" Danny stepped up but Christy stopped him and said, "I can handle this bum." Turning to the young man she said, "I have a better idea! Why don't you go back to your cabin, alone, and forgive yourself?!" The young guy looked at her and blinked. Then he laughed and said, "Oh I get it. Damn lady! You're good! Ok. I'm outta here." Danny laughed as he watched the guy stumble as he walked away. He said to her, "That was priceless! You can not only handle yourself physically with your Martial Arts training but also verbally. I wish I had that one on video." Christy laughed and said, "You have to stand up to these jerks. They're mostly all mouth."

They talked as they walked to her cabin. Danny said, "I'm sorry the evening has to end so soon. I hope it wasn't something I said." Christy answered, "Oh heavens no. I really am tired. I could stay up a while and talk if you want." That alleviated his concerns as he answered, "How about if we just save it for tomorrow? We're at sea all day. How about you and Stacie joining us for breakfast in the dining room at nine o'clock?" She surprised him when she said, "How about nine o'clock just...you and I?" He smiled and said, "It's a date. I'm an early riser so I'll have a cup of coffee while my daughter has her breakfast. We like to get up early and exercise. Ok then, nine o'clock just....you and I."

When they reached her room she said, "Well, here it is. Thank you so much for a pleasant dinner and conversation." Now testing him she said, "I would invite you in but I don't want you or our kids, if they come back early, to get the wrong idea." Danny smiled and thought, 'Ok. I'll pass your test. Now here's my test.' Responding he said, "I totally understand how any man would want to get the wrong idea with such a beautiful woman like you. But I pride myself on being a respectful gentleman with great self control. I assure you, the only thing that would happen if I came in, would only be conversation."

Laughing he continued, "I must say that I maybe a grandfather, but I'm still very much a young *grandfather. You get your rest. And I also thank you for not only a very pleasant dinner, but also for a very pleasant day." Looking into each other's eyes they smiled. Extending his hand to shake hers, he winked and said, "See you in the morning at breakfast, just...*you and I.*"*

He surprised her as she was absolutely positive that he was going to try to give her a goodnight kiss. This was a first time that she experienced someone not making any kind of an advance at her after seeing her home, or in this case, to her cabin. They both passed their tests. Turning and leaving he arrived at his room where he changed into comfortable casual clothes before taking a tour of the ship.

While he was in his cabin changing his clothes, Danny thought, 'Holy Jeez! For the second time this year it didn't take me any time at all to get that queasy feeling in the pit of my stomach for someone I just met. First it's Pretty Cowgirl. Now it's Christy. Man oh man! She's gorgeous and I know I usually take things slow but I don't know why the hell I want to go faster with her. *God I hope I'm not getting desperate. I'm gonna get a drink and think this over.'*

After leaving his cabin, he went to the piano bar where he sat at the bar, ordered a scotch, and sat there listening to the piano player while sipping his drink. Along came a middle aged blonde woman who sat next to him and ordered a drink as well. She had a hidden agenda. She was an oversexed woman who wanted Danny the minute he walked into the place. Making her move she started a casual conversation. He was never rude so he engaged in the chat. Sitting in the back of the room and now watching were Vicky and Stacie.

Stacie said, "What the hell does she think she's doing?" Vicky said, "That's not unusual. I've seen it before many times. Wherever my dad goes, there is usually some stage-five-clinger *trying to attach them self to him. Don't worry. When he senses it he cuts it off and leaves." Stacie said, "That's too funny. It happens to my mom all the time too." They laughed when Vicky said, "Sometimes guys come up to him. Those are the ones that throw him off. Usually dad just says, no thanks, and the guy backs off and walks away. But when they don't and they get persistent, then he gets really pissed. That's when they get the message to leave, or else." Stacie said, "Same thing with my mom. She can speak sailor's language when she gets pissed at someone who won't stop pestering her. But then she had to learn to do that when guys get aggressive with her. Oh oh! What's she doing now? Oh crap on Friday. She's making a move on your dad."*

On that cue, Danny stood up and left the bar. The woman quickly finished her drink before walking out after him. The girls watched her standing outside the bar looking around for about thirty seconds before throwing both hands up and walking away frustrated. As they focused their attention on her they were startled by a man's low voice requesting them to make room for him to sit down. Their heads snapped back and they let out a nervous laugh until they realized it was Danny. He said, "I saw you two here and I didn't want to bother you. When that woman got to the point where she whispered some nasty garbage in my ear I told her to get lost and decided to make my exit. Before I left I spotted an Employees Only *sign over the door behind the piano player. When I left I made a bee line for the other room and came in to join you here while she looks around for me. Gotta have a little fun with these idiots. Sorry to interrupt your conversation. All I wanted was a scotch before going back to my cabin." Stacie said, "That was hilarious Mr. Can...I mean Danny. I didn't expect to see you here. I thought you were going to spend some time with mom." Danny answered, "I walked her to her room. She's tired and needs her rest. I'm surely not gonna bother anyone when they're tired. Your mom is gorgeous, sweet, and very interesting but I'm not selfish. When a woman says she needs some rest...she needs some rest. Well, I'm gonna go now. I hope the coast is clear." Finishing his scotch he reached over, picked up their tab,* and paid for their drinks. Before leaving for his cabin, he gave his daughter a kiss on her cheek first, then while shaking Stacie's hand he smiled and made firm eye contact with her, and told them he was going to meet Christy for breakfast at nine.

After watching Danny walk out of the piano bar, Stacie turned to Vicky and said, "Holy crap! Your dad melted my heart! If my mom doesn't take him...I will! Hope you don't mind having a younger step-mom!" Laughing Vicky responded, "Not at all. I just hope you're not mean to your step-daughter. Hahaha!" Returning the wit Stacie said, "I won't be as long as you mind what I tell you. Hahaha! Hey Vicky. The way they looked at dinner I bet you one thing for sure. I bet both of them will be taking a cold shower tonight." Vicky shook her head, laughed, and said, "I wouldn't doubt that at all...step-grandma!" Stacie said, "Oh crap! I didn't think about that. Oh what the hell, Ok!"

Back in his room Danny stepped out of the shower and dressed for bed. He thought, 'Damn the cold water on this boat is really cold. Brrrr! Now I've got to get on my app and play a few games with my poker partner. Hope she's on. I have to know if this encounter with Christy today changed my feelings for Pretty Cowgirl.'

The ship provided free Wi-Fi for all its passengers. After changing and getting into bed, he turned on his phone, logged onto the game and started to play. Within about ten minutes he received an invitation from Pretty Cowgirl for a private game. Accepting the invitation he joined the table and they began to play and chat. From their conversation, to both of them, it was the same feeling. They both still felt very attracted to each other. Now, they also felt a little confused but both thought the same thing as they smiled a lot during their time playing online together. Now they figured they had a choice with potentially two relationships. For the next hour, they played, had a deep conversation, and poked fun at each other like they normally did before closing out the game with heartfelt pleasant messages.

Chapter 13
Day 2 - Breakfast

At *six a.m. the next morning Vicky answered the knocking at her cabin door. Knowing it was her dad she opened the door and told him she was up late last night and would skip the early breakfast and work out. He understood and went on by himself to get a short jog around the trail on the top deck before going to the weight room and then the steam room. Feeling very invigorated after a shower, he sat in the restaurant waiting for Christy, and checked his e-mails while enjoying a cup of coffee. At 8:45 a.m. she walked into the room and up to his table. Danny was so involved in reading his messages that he did not notice her standing about five feet away from him until she cleared her throat and got his attention. Looking up he did a double take.*

She was wearing stylish cut off blue jeans and a short sleeve loose shirt over her bathing suit, and a sun visor around her forehead. Danny thought, 'Oh wow! She looks so sexy and gorgeous in anything.' Danny stood, greeted her, and waited until she was seated before taking his seat and putting away his cell phone. He wore shorts and a polo shirt and she thought, 'This guy looks amazing at any hour of the day!' The waiter pulled her chair for her to sit and join him.

Danny said, "I hope you got a good night's sleep." Christy answered, "Yes thanks. I hope you had a good workout this morning after breakfast with your daughter." He laughed and said, "She never made it to breakfast. I assume your daughter didn't either since I saw them out together last night." Christy laughed saying, "I couldn't budge her this morning. They must have stayed out late last night. I didn't even hear her come in. Glad to see she made a friend with Vicky. She's a good kid and I worry sometimes about who she's out with." He answered, "I know what you mean. And you should be. You know that we struggle to protect our kids when we raise them. And when they grow up you believe the worst is behind you, only to realize that little kids present little problems, and big kids present big problems. Let me assure you that Stacie is in good hands. (laughing) And I feel good knowing that Vicky has a bodyguard with a Black Belt!" Laughing as she responded she said, "She sure knows how to defend herself alright. When she was in high school, on her way home one day, a boy hit her on the school bus and she flattened him. She never got suspended but the boy did and he was glad for one thing. He was glad he did NOT *have to show his face at school for a week. Well how about some breakfast?"*

The conversation continued as they ate their morning meal. Danny was pleased that Christy asked him for a private breakfast together and he told her so. He said, "I'm glad you suggested this. I hope I'm not being too forward when I tell you that after I had such a good time yesterday I really wanted to get to know you better. I haven't had anyone close in my life since Rachel passed away and anyone I've met since then...well let's say nothing worked out. Besides the tournament, and time with my daughter this cruise is also a change of scenery after a few bad experiences."

Christy said, "You're not being forward at all. As a matter of fact, that's why I suggested this. We have more in common now. Besides the tournament, and time with my daughter, I needed this to get away from some of the people around me too. And I agree, after yesterday, and after you showed me last night what a decent man you seem to be, I want to get to know you better too. Just between me and you...Stacie thinks you're the bomb*!" He scratched his head and asked, "What's* the bomb*?" She laughed and answered, "That's her generation's word for;* you're absolutely handsome and desirable." *He laughed and said, "Well thank you and tell her she's a sweetheart and* a bomb *as well!"*

The conversation moved to more serious topics about their lives. The more they revealed and got to know about each other, the more they developed stronger emotionally about each other. They actually fought off deeper feelings believing it was way too early and too quick for this to be happening to them.

She asked about his life with Rachel and what he thought was the secret for their strong relationship. He said, "Coincidentally, someone asked me that years ago while Rachel and I were on a cruise. I guess they were expecting me to say something like communication, or trust, because she was so damn beautiful that they thought I probably couldn't do any better. I think it shocked the hell out of them when I said that I can sum that up in one word: unselfishness. *That one thing encompasses everything in a strong relationship. Love, trust, fidelity, honor, friendship, communication. Everything. Whatever we did, we thought of the other person first. That made it so easy."*

Hearing his explanation Christy's heart pounded. She thought, 'Wow. He sure got to me with that too.' He asked, "How about you? What kept you and John going so strong all those years? Sounds like you found what I found."

Turning away for a moment to contain her emotions she turned back and said, "Yes. I never could define it before, but what you said makes a lot of sense. John and I married early. We knew each other since junior high school. He always made me feel special and he did everything he could to make me happy. Which was pretty easy since I'm very satisfied with anything good someone does for me. We also thought of each other first and never let anyone or anything come between us. Not our child or anyone. Funny thing was, when I met John I thought I was young and homely. He was strong and handsome. He told me that I was the most beautiful girl he ever saw and that there was also a gorgeous woman inside of me that really got to him. At first I didn't believe him. But he treated me with genuine love and respect and made me feel like the queen of his castle."

Looking away for a few seconds she wiped her eyes and continued, "Unfortunately this fairly tale did not have a good ending." She was a little red eyed when she looked up at Danny. Feeling empathy for her he said, "Yes. I too know that ending all too well. But looking at the brighter side it looks like we both have something that many never had. Some even after thirty, forty, or fifty years of marriage. We have an incredible experience that many others only hear about from people like you and me." That made her feel better.

Now he looked away for a few seconds before turning back to her and saying, "It's a crying shame that I lost my queen and you lost your king. So what do we do now?" Trying to add levity she snickered and said, "Well. I guess we play poker!" Turning serious she added, "Let me just say. I still want to continue our conversations and have some more breakfasts together. But I have to confess something. There is another person in my life right now, and before we move any faster or closer, I've got to see if there's something more there." Danny spoke up and said, "Yes. I was gonna say something as well but you beat me to it. I also have someone I wanna follow up with. And it's only fair to both of you, and to me, to do that. My brain always tells me to take a relationship slow, and I don't know why, but now my heart's telling me to move faster. My brain is usually right."

Laughing she answered, "I'm not laughing at you. I'm laughing because I remember that I reminded my daughter about a man's brain a while ago. I'll let her tell you what her dad shared with her about his wisdom regarding a man's brain. Sorry but it's funny and she never forgot it." Returning the laugh he said, "It's probably the same thing I told Vicky and my son Chris about too. It's an old joke but it has a lot of truth about blood flow. Am I right?" Blushing and laughing Christy answered, "Absolutely! Well on another note, I've got to go. I promised Stacie I would spend the afternoon with her before getting ready for the tournament tonight. She seemed pretty anxious for me to take my time with you at breakfast."

As she stood up to leave, Danny stood up and asked, "That reminded me of something that I forgot to ask you. We're both poker players and we can read people pretty well right?" She nodded in agreement. He continued, "I have a suspicion that we have a couple of young ladies here that may be manipulating their time so that we can spend some time together privately. Did you pick up on that?"

She answered, "You mean when they didn't think we noticed how they were mimicking us walking to our table last night and then giving a silent high five? Yes I believe they are." He laughed and said, "I saw that too. Also how they did the same when we were walking to our room yesterday afternoon and they were behind us. I saw them in the mirror as we walked down the stairs. Do you want to get them back? I mean in a fun way. We can act like we're not interested every time they try to get us together. Just until the tournament is over in three days. I don't want to ruin their fun time on the cruise." They both laughed when Christy smiled and said, "I'm All In!" They continued to laugh when Danny answered, "Call!"

Before leaving the dining room Danny extended his hand to Christy. As they stood there shaking hands their smiles disappeared as they stared deeply into each others' eyes. Before leaving Christy said, "I want a hug." Danny's heart raced as he said, "I want one too!" as he obliged her by embracing her tightly for a few seconds *before letting go and holding both her hands. This was what they both needed.*

He could not help himself as he stood there and watched her as she walked all the way to the dining room door. She turned and seeing him staring at her she winked and blew him a kiss before turning and walking out. Standing there smiling he thought, 'I hope she's not at any of my tables during the tournament. It's gonna take all the self control I have just to focus on the game.'

Chapter 14
The Tournament Begins

Later *that evening after dinner with only his daughter, Danny talked about his day. Vicky was very curious about how his breakfast with Christy went. Keeping to his scheme he answered, "Oh it went ok. Nothing special. She's a beauty but I'm not really finding as many things in common as I thought I would." That surprised and concerned his daughter and made her feel terrible. It drained her smile and brought a serious look to her face. She tried to act like it wasn't a problem and said, "Dad. It's really early. You don't know much about her yet. Why don't you try a little harder? That look on your face when you first saw her was something I didn't see since mom was alive." Knowing he couldn't hide everything he responded, "Oh c'mon hun. Sure she's beautiful. But looks aren't everything. There has to be more, and I'm not seeing it yet. Ok. I'll try harder! But no promises."*

She shook her head at him and finally deciding to tell him she said, "Don't tell her I told you this, but Stacie told me last night that you melted her heart, and if her mom doesn't want you, then she'll take you...now!" Laughing he said, "What? C'mon." Jokingly he continued, "That's very sweet and flattering of her, but what am I gonna do with her? She's younger than you. Can you imagine what the Board of Directors and their wives would think of me? I'd probably get fired!" She said, "I know dad. I'm sure she didn't mean it that way."

He turned to her and said, "Listen honey. I appreciate all you do for me. Just let me figure things out when it comes time to Christy. I really appreciate what you're trying to tell me and if I need your advice, I promise, I will ask. Fair enough? Now I have to concentrate on the tournament and I don't want to lose my focus."

Vicky smiled, then winked at him and said, "Ok dad. Fair enough." Finishing her dinner she thought, 'Wow. Here's a gorgeous goddess of a single woman that I see has a heart of gold, and my dad's focus is on poker? Oh shit! Did those dates with Peggy, Cathy, and Simone mess him up that bad? I sure hope not! I have to talk to Stacie!' Finishing his supper before getting up to go to his cabin to change his clothes for the tournament, he saw the concerned look on Vicky, and thought, 'Hahaha. I see this is driving her crazy. I bet she's thinking that I've gone off the deep end with relationships.'

The tournament was sold out one month before the ship sailed. Half of the casino located on the Promenade Deck was roped off and set up with twenty poker tables that accommodated seven players on each for a total of one hundred forty participants. The scheduled beginning time of the tournament was eight o'clock. The time limit placed on the Day 1 tournament was four hours. At the end of play the top seventy players with the most chips moved on to Day 2. The rules were explained to all the players before play started and those rules were also posted at each table in plain sight. The game was played according to the standard poker hand rankings and standard rules for playing no-limit Texas Hold 'em.

Seating was randomly set up ahead of time by the casino referee group. Danny and Christy were relieved to see that they were not seated at the same table. After the rule briefing, the dealers unwrapped brand new decks of cards, and placing them in a machine to their left, the cards were automatically counted, shuffled, and ready to deal. The dealer's job is to deal the cards correctly and ensure the bets are completed before moving on.

Texas Hold 'em is played by first dealing two cards face down to each player. Betting begins with these first two face down cards. After that, the dealer places the community cards in front of him or her. Community cards are the next five cards, face up, that the players can use along with their two, face down, cards to make the best five card hand. The dealer first deals three of the community cards, face up, in front of him. Those first cards dealt are called 'The Flop.' Betting continues. Then the dealer turns another card, face up, to go with the three cards. Again, the betting continues. That fourth card is called 'The Turn' card. Betting continues. Then the dealer deals the fifth and last card face up, called 'The River' card. Here is where the betting is final. If the game reached this point, and the betting is completed, the players reveal their cards, in what's called the 'Showdown,' where the winner is determined.

About an hour into the tournament, Danny had taken a strong lead at his table and ranked eighth in overall play. Christy is struggling but doing fair and ranked thirty fourth. Needing to be in the top seventy for Day 1 was making her a little nervous. She started off winning a sizable pot on her first hand. However, she had to fold with very poor hole cards in the next three rounds of play. That put her in an uncomfortable position.

The third hour had Danny in a comfortable spot ranking in the top ten while Christy was still struggling and now in fifty third place. Danny felt bad seeing her struggle but there was obviously nothing he could do. Focusing on his play he decided to coast and not take any big chances as play continued into the fourth hour.

Now into the final ten minutes of play, Danny was in seventh place while Christy was sweating it out with another player for sixty eighth place. During the final hand at her table, three of the players who were all fighting for final spots, were betting high. Being in that last match brought her chip count down below the amount needed to qualify for Day 2. If she lost, she was out. Danny watched since he already qualified and folded his last hand. Christy flinched as she looked at her hole cards and the others at the table saw that. They called "All In" and each one felt confident they had at least a better hand than her. She had no choice but to "Call" their bet and put the rest of her chips into the pot. With a blank stare she looked on as each person before her turned over their hole cards.

The first one had a spade flush. The second player frowned as he showed three of a kind. The third player smiled as she turned over her hole cards revealing a higher spade flush. Christy looked at her opponent with the higher flush and broke her blank stare as she turned over her hole cards. She had four of a kind and fooled them all. After all the frustration of struggling with poor hole cards she was relieved to know that she made it to *fifty ninth place and was going to the second round. She looked up and saw Danny smiling and cheering.*

Chapter 15
Sun, Fun, Tournament Day 2

It *was about nine a.m. the next morning when Vicky met her dad in the dining room for breakfast. Last night after the tournament, he told her before he left her and Stacie at the piano bar that he would let her sleep in and to join him at around nine. The ship was docked in the port of Freeport, Bahamas that morning. It was the first of the two ports on the cruise itinerary. The excursion they had planned today was a two hour swimming with and feeding the dolphins. They selected the eleven o'clock time so they would have plenty of time to get back to the ship, relax, and have dinner before round two of the tournament began.*

Noticing her dad only ordered coffee Vicky asked, "Hey dad. Is coffee all you're having? He nods. She continues, "You did really well last night. Dad I really appreciate you spending time with me, but I'm sort of down that you're not spending more time with Christy."

Danny thought to himself, 'If you only knew that I was up at six a.m. with Christy to watch the sunrise, and later had breakfast with her! But I'll let her sweat it out another day.' He then answered her saying, "I'm absolutely fine. I was up earlier, watched a beautiful sunrise, had breakfast, worked out, and now I'm enjoying a cup of coffee with my favorite daughter." Laughing she said, "You always said that and I still laugh at it. I'm your only daughter and you're a real schmoozer dad. You tell Chris he's your favorite son, and Donna that she's your favorite daughter-in-law. I love it dad. I just wish you weren't watching the sunrise alone." He said, "Ok. I'll make you a deal."

Vicky now smiling was anticipating her dad's comment. He said, "Tomorrow. I'll make it a point to watch the sunrise with my favorite daughter!" She squinted her eyes at him and said, "C'mon dad. You know who I'm talking about." He said, "Ok. I'll take Stacie with me then. Since she thinks I'm the bomb!" She laughed and said, "What? She said that? How do you know?" He answered, "Don't tell her I know but that's what Christy told me when we had breakfast. I didn't know what the hell a bomb *was before she explained it to me." With a serious look on her face she said, "C'mon dad. Keep trying with Christy. If you don't ask her, then I will!" He said, "Fine. You can ask her to watch the sunrise with you. That's fine with me. I'm just kidding. Ok. If it means that much to you, then I'll ask her. Or maybe you should ask her for me." Pointing to the front of the dining room he said, "Look. There they are. Go ahead and ask."*

Containing his laughter, he watched his daughter quickly stand up and head straight for the women at the door. Before a waiter attended to them Vicky ushered them to the table where they sat down with her and her dad. Standing for the ladies to take their seats, Danny greeted them saying, "Hello again lovely ladies. Stacie? I trust you got to sleep in this morning." Stacie looked around and said, "Yes sir. I needed that. Vicky and I made some friends with a group of people and we laughed and danced until almost three o'clock this morning. I could probably use some more sleep but we have the eleven o'clock dolphin thing to go to and I'm pretty excited." Vicky spoke up and said, "That's great. We have the same excursion and I'm excited about that too. We even brought some underwater cameras. I can't wait."

Danny cut into the conversation and said, "Well I was up early. When Vicky was a child she was a night owl and stayed up as long as she could. I used to tell everyone that sometimes I wake up grumpy, and sometimes I let her sleep in. She would get mad at me for saying that. Anyway, I enjoyed seeing the beautiful sunrise this morning." Danny looked at Christy and said,

"Oh by the way, Christy. My daughter wants to ask you something."

Shaking her head Vicky glared at her dad, then turned to Christy and said, "Christy? I noticed some strange and scary people on this cruise. Would you do me a great big favor and accompany my dad, for his protection of course, tomorrow morning while he watches the beautiful sunrise? I would feel much better knowing you would protect him from all those scary people. Please?*"*

They all laughed at her request. Christy looked at Vicky and responded, "Well, he appears to be a little helpless. And I know what you mean about some of the suspiciously strange characters aboard the ship. (laughing) I noticed some blonde haired middle aged woman stalking him too. I sure don't want him to get hurt in any way. And seeing that it will make you sleep in better, and not wake up grumpy...well, OK." Christy thought, 'If these two kids only knew where I was this morning while that sun was coming up. And if Danny only knew how much I wanted to jump in that Jacuzzi with him, and place a huge kiss on his lips, I think we might be out there until the sun went down!' Vicky looked over at Stacie and winked. Stacie smiled back and nodded. After breakfast they agreed to meet later at the dolphin encounter.

After the dolphin excursion they boarded the ship and went back to their respective cabins to shower and change. Vicky and Stacie walked separately and quietly conversed. Danny had to take another cold shower after seeing Christy in an incredibly sexy bikini, which he did not know she wore that especially for him. Regardless, they had fun. Christy also had a difficult time keeping her eyes off of Danny's nicely sculpted body that went with his handsome face. Their daughters giggled every time they caught Danny or Christy sneaking a stare at the other. Stacie's thoughts raced to imagining that it felt like a family with a new dad and a best friend for a sister. She kept that to herself as she didn't want to say anything that she felt would pressure her mom.

Stepping into the bathroom to take a shower after her mom, Stacie laughed as she said, "No fog? I guess the ship ran out of hot water mom." Giving her mom a sly smile she continued, "He's a hottie isn't he mom?" Christy laughed as she responded, "Ok. Don't be a smart ass. And yes, he is a hottie. And the bomb. And yes, the ship ran out of hot water too!" Afterwards, they dressed and went to the Lido Deck to get some sun, and enjoy their mother-daughter time together.

Vicky showered, called home to check on Stephen and her son, then laid down to take a much needed two hour nap.

Danny went to the ship's library to be alone and think. Ordering a scotch he sat at the table and looked out the window. He thought, 'It's only been a few days now and I'm feeling things I haven't felt since Rachel. This is scary. What's even scarier is I can't take my mind off of Christy and I can't stop thinking about Pretty Cowgirl either. This doesn't make any sense at all. Oh man, how much I wanted to hug her, and kiss her, and take her back to my cabin and make passionate love to her this morning. But that's not like me so early on and I know I'd lose her for sure. Oh damn! I'm usually never at a loss for a game plan. Now I don't know what to do. I'll admit it's a great place to be in, but I sure don't want to screw anything up by making a wrong move. Maybe I should open up to Pretty Cowgirl and get everything out in the open. No. No, I mustn't rush anything. I'll have to take my time and take my chances. What a damned dilemma. I feel like I wish I could have both of them. What a dumb thought.'

Both couples had an early dinner since they skipped lunch. Danny sat at the table with a faraway look in his eyes. Seeing her father was distant, quiet, and somewhat melancholy, Vicky broke the silence and said, "The food on these cruises is great and they really do a good job pampering you." Nodding he said, "Yes they do."

Seeing she was getting nowhere with small talk she asked, "Ok dad. What's bothering you? You've been distant for the last hour and now you look like you're lost in space. You can tell me. What's up? I know it's not the poker match." That brought a grin to his face. Opening up he said, "This has to stay between me and you. Promise me that?" With a serious look she shook her head yes. He continued, "You see, I have a dilemma and I don't want to do anything to mess things up." She asked, "All the years I've known you, you've always managed to work your way out of any issue you or mom had. What's the dilemma that seems to be overwhelming you?"

He said, "After Rachel, I've always taken things slowly and methodically when it came time to relationships. This worked for me because taking time allowed me to notice any bad patterns in a person before deciding whether I wanted to move on with that person or not. Some people it was early on and others it took longer. I know it hasn't been long since your mom passed and it's a little daunting at the thought of another person. Especially in light of my last few experiences. What gems those were! *But now I find myself wanting to shift it into fifth gear with two women!"*

Vicky said, "Two women? I can see that one is Christy. But please dad, don't tell me the other is that Pretty Girl, or whatever her name is from that online game. That's crazy! You don't know anything about her! I don't understand that at all." He answered, "I didn't think you would because, I don't understand it either! *I never thought anything like this would ever happen. Especially on this cruise. I'm really falling for Christy. But I'm also falling for Pretty Cowgirl too! I know it sounds crazy. So I decided I'm going to open up to Pretty Cowgirl after the tournament and find out who she is. Then I'm gonna take it from there. What do you think?"*

Vicky answered, "That's a good idea. This way you should get an answer while you still have a couple of days left on the cruise with Christy. You were right again dad." He asked, "Right again? About what?" She answered, "Remember when we asked you if you wanted to meet this Pretty Cowgirl on the cruise? You were right when you said: No Way!. *Can you imagine what it would be like to have both of them here?" He shook his head and laughed saying, "That would be an even greater dilemma. I'd probably wind up jumping overboard!"*

Day 2 of the tournament was only fifteen minutes away from starting in the roped off area of the casino. Tonight there were ten tables set up with seven players at each table. The four hour time limit began sharply at eight o'clock. This time it was the top thirty five players at the end of four hours who would move on to the Day 3, which was the final elimination match. The large crowd gathered in an area about ten feet behind the players who were already seated at their assigned tables.

Once again, Christy and Danny were seated at different tables. After the first hour of play the ranking boards showed Danny and Christy in the top ten. Both were playing masterfully. Christy was finally relieved to receive hole cards that were decent enough to play as opposed to the horrible cards she was dealt the night before.

Christy was feeling more confident tonight. Not only due to her play but also from today's dolphin encounter with Danny and the girls. At the table she had a couple of men who seemed to be paying more attention to her low cut red blouse than they did to their poker hands. In three rounds she managed to win all their chips since they were distracted by her sensuality. They thought she was bluffing on one occasion when she winked at one of them. She revealed a full house in the third hand when both of them went All In. They said things like, "Oh crap. I knew I had you beat," and "You really fooled me." She smiled and answered, "Thank you gentleman. See you again at the next tournament." Now three hours passed and she and Danny were still in the top ten.

Coming to the close of the match on Day 2 were easy victories in chip counts for Danny and Christy. They ranked more than high enough to qualify for Day 3 along with thirty three other players. They stood up and shook each other's hand as they walked off to the piano bar for *a celebratory drink before heading off to their cabins for a much needed night sleep.*

Vicky and Stacie stopped to talk a while and tried to come up with another scheme to keep Christy and Danny seeing as much of each other as possible. Then they met up with their newfound group of friends and went to clubs. After finishing their drinks Danny walked Christy to her cabin. This time when they reached her cabin she said, "I want you to come in for a minute please." He agreed and, after entering, Christy secured the door so no one could enter without first knocking. She turned to him and said, "I just wanted to see you alone for a minute. I've never done this before and I don't want to lose my nerve so just bear with me. I just want to kiss you. Nothing more right now and I'm not taking no for an answer."

He smiled and said, "I want to kiss you too but I wanted the time to be right. I wanted to wait until the sunrise tomorrow and ask you, but I don't think I can wait any longer either." With that they embraced and kissed passionately for about ten seconds. They both let out a soft, "Ahh" and a moan and kissed again. Then they stood there in a tight embrace looking into each other's eyes while caressing each other's back.

Stepping back he picked up her hand, kissed it, and said, "I think it's time for me to go. Believe me when I *say that was great! And while my body says stay, my mind says go...*for now.*" She responded, "Same here. That was better than I imagined too. I'll let you go...*for now. *For my sake I just hope the ship's shower water is very cold tonight. This will be my third one." Laughing he said, "Yes. It's cold alright. I can vouch for it. This is my third one too!" Walking out of her cabin he went straight to his cabin, shut the door, took another cold shower, and went to bed with a great big smile on his face that lasted all night.*

Chapter 16
Vicky's Surprise &
Tournament Day 3

Sunrise *was at six fifteen a.m. as Danny and Christy, with their arms around each other's waist, watched it slowly rise above the eastern horizon from the top deck of the ship. Then they stood there, lost in each other's embrace, and kissed after the sun came into full view. Danny paid one of the ship's photographers to capture those moments. He snapped beautiful pictures of them silhouetted against the sun. The one that came out the best was the one of them where their lips were just about to meet as a glimmer of sunlight separated the moment of contact. It looked like a perfect postcard or a Valentine's Day card. It was a great way to begin their day. They developed deep feelings for each other but suppressed them for the time being. At least until the time it took for them to discover the identity of their online fantasy partner.*

After a short breakfast, where they did less talking, and more gazing into each other's eyes, he walked her to her room. Before leaving for his cabin they engaged in a long passionate kiss and strong firm embrace. Afterwards, he told her he would see her later that night at the tournament. The ship had already left Freeport from the night before, and was on its way for a two day sailing to Grand Cayman Island. Danny and Christy thought it would be best if they spent most of those next two days separately with their own daughter since they felt they had been neglecting them.

Going back to his room Danny was wide awake as he laid in bed. At this point he brushed away his guilty feelings of blazing into a new relationship and embraced the excitement he felt for Christy. He was anxious though, about wanting to open up to his online fantasy woman Pretty Cowgirl, so he took out his phone and logged onto the game. He played and waited for about twenty minutes but checking his tagged friends every so often, he didn't see her. Just as he was ready to sign out of the app she appeared and sent him an invitation to play in a private game. Smiling and getting that good feeling in the pit of his stomach he thought, 'Good. Now I'm ready to see who my Pretty Cowgirl really is.'

After exchanging greetings Danny read a message from her that stunned him. Pretty Cowgirl wrote, 'Clint. I believe we have both been open and honest so I hope you understand what I'm going to share with you.' He responded, 'Go on. I'm listening. By your statement it doesn't sound like it's going to be good.' She said, 'I'm upset and crying right now because I don't know how to tell you.' He messaged, 'It's ok. Just say what's on your mind. I'm a big boy. I've had my heart broken before. And I think it may be tested again.' She messaged, 'I can't explain my feelings but hear me out please. For the last month I felt that I was falling in love with you. Recently I found another man. And now both of you have won my heart and I don't know what to do. I've never met you but you've been kind, and gentle, and even helped me feel beautiful without ever seeing me. This man saw me and makes me feel the same way. I'm very confused. If I could, I wish I could take both of you, but I know that sounds crazy and it's not fair. I want some time to think and I want to open up to you in a couple of days so that we can see who each other really is. Would you do that for me please?'

Danny thought, 'Wow. She's hurting just like I am and I want the same thing.' He messaged back, 'Before I met you I was the kind of man who always took a relationship slow. Since I met you, I can't believe it either, but I found myself wanting to go faster than I ever imagined. I understand what you're saying. I too feel like I've fallen in love with you. And yes it sounds crazy. But it's true. Please don't be upset. And I agree. I want us to reveal ourselves to each other also. In a couple of days is fine with me. What do you say we get in touch through this game in two days at twelve midnight my Pretty Cowgirl?'

Christy smiled as she wiped her eyes and typed, 'I'll be waiting, my handsome Clint. Bye for now.' He messaged, 'It's a date. See you then.' Shutting off their app both of them, sighed and then stared at the ceiling lost in their thoughts. Finally both of them drifted off to nap for a couple of hours.

Stacie and Vicky were eating breakfast and giggling as they talked about eavesdropping on Christy and Danny while they were watching the sunrise. They laughed and gave themselves all the credit for matching them up. Stacie, in all her excitement didn't realize what she blurted out when she said, "I'm so glad they're together. Good job girl! Now maybe my mom could drop this other guy she's been whining about on the web that she never even met."

Vicky was wise. Hearing this made her stop to fully digest what she just heard. She hesitated and thought it through thoroughly before fishing for more information by saying, "Yeah. Well I guess she has a lot of guys after her and I don't blame them. That's weird though. Who is this guy she never met? What does he look like? And do you know him? Tell me. I'm curious."

Stacie opened up, "Well I guess mom wouldn't mind since she doesn't have anything to hide. She probably told your dad about him, but I'm not saying anything to her, because I don't want to get in the middle of their relationship. It's some random guy she met online while playing some dumb poker game on her cell phone."

Hearing this Vicky was stunned. She felt like her heart stopped beating for a second. Stacie continued, "Mom ran into all kinds of morons who wanted to date her. But all they wanted was sex. Those guys turned her off and made her feel like a nasty piece of meat for these rabid dogs. So she decided to stop dating for a while. Well she started playing this game on her phone. That's where she met this guy. I thought she was just wasting her time playing with him all hours of the night. She told me that he's sweet and kind to her. Well of course he is! He obviously can't reach through the phone and grab her like the other guys try to do. Maybe he's honest. I don't know. For what it's worth, to his credit, this guy seems to calm her down, make her laugh, and make her feel really good all over. She calls him her fantasy man."

Outwardly Vicky was very calm, cool, collected, and attentive. But inwardly she was erupting and trembling with excitement. Here was her opening. She had to know. Is this guy or isn't he her dad? Hiding the nervousness from her anticipation Vicky responded, "Wow. It sounds like my dad has some tough competition." Then she asked, "Does this guy live near you? Do you know his name?"

Not catching on to Vicky's nervousness Stacie answered, "She doesn't know anything about his identity or where he lives. All she knows is he goes by the name of Clint." Vicky's thought blasted in her head, 'OH...MY...GOD!!! IT **IS** DAD!!!' To put the full stamp of confirmation on this she asked, "That's so weird Stacie. Does he know who your mom is?" Holding her breath she waited for an answer. Stacie replied, "No. She won't tell him yet. When they play together, all he knows is, she goes by the name of Pretty Cowgirl. Isn't that a scream?"

Vicky drank her water to keep from fainting or screaming at the top of her lungs. Trying to hold in her exhilaration, she faked feeling sleepy, and yawned. Then laughing she said, "Yeah. That's a scream all right! Well. I guess I'm gonna go back to my cabin and get a couple hours of sleep. We're burning the candle at both ends and it's really catching up with me. I don't want to have to take a vacation to recuperate from this vacation."

Laughing, Stacie said, "Yeah. Me too. I think I'll go out on the Lido Deck, take a nap, and get a suntan at the same time. Ok Vicky. I'll see you later." Both young ladies stood up, gave each other a hug and a high five before turning and going their own way. Once Stacie was out of sight, Vicky ran down the stairs to her cabin, where *she sat down on her bed to catch her breath and try to calm down as she was trembling with excitement. All the while she was thinking of what to do now that she was the only one who knew the true identities of Clint and Pretty Cowgirl!*

Vicky was so excited she couldn't think straight. She became very frustrated with the fact that she knew something so huge in her dad's life that she didn't know what to do with the information. Finally she threw up her hands and said, "Oh hell! Whenever I had a problem dad was always there to help me. So I'll do what I always do and bring it up to him." She took a few deep breaths, then drank a bottle of water before stepping out of her cabin, and over to her dad's room. She was still visibly shaking from the anxiety of the meeting. She took a few more deep breaths before knocking on his door.

It took about ten knocks on the door before Danny woke up. He shouted, "Just a minute!" as he stood up from the bed, yawned, stretched, and walked over to the door. Rubbing his eyes as he opened the door he said, "Oh hey hun." Seeing the expression on her face concerned him. With a stern look he said, "Are you OK? What's wrong? You lost all the color in your face. Come in and sit down."

Vicky shook her head, and at a loss for words, just walked in and took a seat. Danny sat down on the bed and looking at her through his squinted eyes he asked, "What's wrong sweetheart?" Vicky realized she better open up and said, "Dad? I found out something earlier today and I don't know how to tell you." Danny was not one to worry about anything without first getting the facts. He asked, "Ok. Tell me. You know you can tell your dear 'ole dad anything. Is everyone alright at home? What is it?" She shook her head yes and said, "Yeah. Everybody's fine. It has nothing to do with home. I was talking to Stacie earlier and she told me something about Christy."

Danny's mouth dropped and a sudden sharp pain shot through the pit of his stomach. For the first time in a long time, he assumed, and thought the worst before he heard any facts. He thought, 'Oh no. I hope this is not gonna be another bad encounter.' Catching himself he took a few deep breaths and braced himself before saying, "What about Christy?"

Vicky saw the apprehension in her dad and realized her awkwardness caused him needless worry. She quickly snapped out of her daze saying, "Oh sorry dad! It's not a bad thing! I didn't mean to make you worry. I know it's a good thing. I think!" Relieved that the issue was not bad Danny let out a short sigh of relief and said, "Ok. Just go ahead and tell me." Vicky shook her head and said, "Now hold on dad and please contain yourself. What I'm gonna tell you is going to blow...your...mind*! Ready?" He smiled and said, "For crying out loud girl, I've been ready since I let you in. Now c'mon. Quit being so nervous and come out with it!"*

She drew a deep breath and said, "Stacie and I were having breakfast and we were talking about you and her mom and how we spied on you two this morning at sunrise." He said, "Yes I know. I saw you stick your head up a couple of times from behind the bar Sherlock. Go on." She smiled and said, "Well seeing you two holding each other and kissing was so cool. We were both so excited. Then Stacie slipped and said something that floored me. But being a good spy for you, I asked a few probing questions, and she innocently spilled the rest of the beans."

Danny interrupted, "What beans did she spill?" Smiling and now bursting with excitement she said, "Stacie said, seeing how, for the first time, her mom seemed incredibly happy with a man, meaning you, that she wished Christy would drop this other guy in her life." Smiling Danny said, "Well that's nice of Stacie. But she already told me that she had another guy in her life and wanted some time and space. I told her the same thing about me and how I have another woman that I need a little time with too. That's not something new."

Smiling back Vicky said, "Well dad. I know the truth about that other guy." Danny squinted again at her and said, "What truth? What did Stacie tell you about that guy?" She gave him a sly look and said, "That other guy....is.....YOU!"

Danny was now very confused and said, "Have you and Stacie been staying up so late at night and then sitting out in the sun too long? What are you talking about? What do you mean? The other guy is me!"

She stood up and walked over to him, took his hands, and getting her face about six inches away from his face she said, "Stacie told me that Christy started to play a game on her phone a while ago. She met some guy on that game and started a conversation that turned very friendly and then turned very serious for her." Danny's mouth dropped and the blood rushed out of his face. Seeing his expression she continued, "Now dad, it looks like you could use a scotch, or two. Guess what? The name of the guy she met on this online game, and has a serious crush on, is a guy named -----Clint!"

Feeling lightheaded he was almost in a state of shock. Then his body shook like he was sitting in ice water. He sat there staring at Vicky and said, "Ho--ly cr--ap!" Snapping out of his trance and trying to make sense of what he was hearing, he demanded in a serious tone, "Are you sure about this? You wouldn't be making this stuff up and playing a horrible joke on me, would you?"

Shaking her head no she answered, "No joking Dad. I'm serious. And to make sure, I, Sherlock, asked if this guy knew anything about her mom. Stacie answered, the only thing this guy knows is that she goes by the name of Pretty Cowgirl!"

Hearing that sealed it for him. Danny threw himself back against his bed in absolute disbelief and stared at the ceiling for a moment. Vicky broke his state of shock and made him chuckle when she said, "And you asked me, 'where would I go if I met Pretty Cowgirl on the ship?' You told me you might just jump overboard! Hahaha!"

After regaining his composure, he thought for a moment, then sat up quickly and asked, "Does Stacie know anything about me being Clint?" Vicky answered, "Would Sherlock reveal anything before he checked with Scotland Yard? Heck no. She does NOT know anything about Clint. I never said a word. I faked feeling sleepy so I could come back here and talk to you. Did I do the right thing, dad?"

He stood up and hugging his daughter he assured her saying, "Absolutely! This explains everything. I played the game online with her last night. She told me some things that were exactly what I was thinking and hoping for. She was so upset that she had two men, in her life and in her heart, and wished she could have both of them. Do you know what that means?" Shaking her head she said, "I do. Pun intended. (they chuckled) But how are you gonna break it to her, dad? You gonna go to her room now?"

He thought for a moment and said, "No. Let me think about it. This is a delicate matter of the heart. I don't want to do anything that will take her focus off her time with her daughter and with the tournament." He thought for a couple of minutes. Snapping his fingers he said, "Oh, I got it!!! Listen. When we last played online, we agreed that we would reveal our identities the day after tomorrow at midnight. I just thought of a plan. And I need your help and Stacie's help. But I don't want you to tell Stacie until about ten o'clock that night. And she has to keep it a secret and play her part. Ok? Now here it is."

Vicky listened as he outlined his plan and the roles she and Stacie were playing. Taking this in and adding her own touches they were in agreement. High fiving each other afterwards Vicky swore complete silence until Danny gave her the signal that night. Checking the time they both decided to get some sleep, or at least lay down, for a few hours before getting ready for dinner and Day 3 of the poker tournament.

Later on, with all the excitement burning within them, Danny and Vicky found it very difficult to finish half of their dinner. Afterwards they walked to the casino for the final elimination day of the tournament. The roped off area now showed five tables consisting of seven players at each table. Of these thirty five players the rule changed to where the top player from each table moved on to the Day 4 Championship match. Tonight there were no time limits. The match at any table could conceivably last anywhere from one hand or about five minutes, to as long as it took the last player to win. The stakes were high and they were not going to leave the final game up to a time clock. At eight o'clock the players were seated and play began. Danny was extremely relieved to once again play at a different table than Christy.

Within the first few hands Christy was slightly ahead. Despite his mind boggling situation, Danny brought his A game, and was able to completely focus his skills on the match. Within the first hour he managed to claim the first seat at the Championship table after masterful play and taking out his opponents very easily. He won in style with a Royal Flush as his last winning hand and bluffing the last two players into an 'All In' bet.

With the aid of great hole cards in several hands, it took just under two hours for Christy to handily win her seat at the Championship table. Danny was extremely impressed at how she beat out the other six players. After almost three hours of play, all the matches were over, and the five finalists were listed on the board as the audience cheered. They were; Danny Canton from

North Carolina, Bill Smith from New York, Elainy Kazen, also from New York, Christy Darren from Florida, and Alex Manning from Georgia. The finalists exchanged congratulatory handshakes with each other before dispersing and leaving the casino.

Smiling as he walked Christy back to her room, Danny contained his excitement. He kept the subject matter neutral and told her how great she played and how he looked forward to playing against her for the championship. Reaching her room they embraced and engaged in a long sensuous goodnight kiss. Then a second kiss. After that, Danny walked back to his cabin, and retired for the evening. For the next hour he ran through his game plan for tomorrow night's meeting with his Pretty Cowgirl before finally going to sleep.

Chapter 17
Hearts Win!

The *excitement of the Championship match on the final day of the tournament was upon Christy and Danny. Added to that was the anxiety of both of them meeting their fantasy person later that night. Christy's heart was pounding out of her chest in anticipation while Danny's heart was racing with the excitement of hoping his plan worked to perfection. Regardless of having only three hours of sleep, Vicky was running on adrenaline when she woke up early enough to join her dad for breakfast. He emphasized the need for secrecy until he gave her, her cue, to open up to Stacie and get her involved. Vicky's job was to record the event and Stacie's job was to encourage and shadow her mom.*

They laughed when Danny said, "Now it's gonna take two Sherlocks to get this job done. I hope it plays out as great as I expect it to! And I hope you get it all on camera. I just hope nothing backfires." Vicky replied, "Don't worry dad. I've got a feeling I'm gonna have my hands full containing Stacie when I tell her about you. That girl is so head over heels about you. She told me, confidentially, that you remind her so much of the way her dad was. Kind, gentle, witty, and good looking. I just hope she doesn't get too nervous and mess things up. But I'm sure everything will go well." They laughed as they finished their breakfast. About twenty minutes after their meal they headed to the ship's exercise room to work off as much of their built up anxiety as possible.

After completing their workout, and a twenty minute stay in separate steam rooms, they showered, before joining Christy and Stacie on the top deck, called the Majestic Deck, to lay out in the sun. They made some small talk, but used this as quiet time together to get caught up on reading and relaxation. However, Vicky and Danny also used this time to review the layout of the deck for their plan.

It was smooth sailing with a mild breeze, eighty degrees, and not a cloud in the sky. Danny and Christy enjoyed putting sun screen on each other and each one was very discreet and respectful. Their daughters acted like they were sitting back and daydreaming, but all the while, behind their dark sunglasses, they stealthily observed and internalized their joy and laughter, as they watched Danny and Christy act as giddy as elementary school kids. Vicky thought, 'I haven't seen my dad this *happy since he enjoyed times like this with mom.' Stacie thought, 'I haven't seen mom this happy with another man since dad. Oh I sure hope she comes to her senses and dumps that Clint guy tonight. If she does anything and loses Danny, she'll never hear the end of it from me! God I wish I could find someone twenty years younger just like him!'*

It was now seven o'clock and all five finalists gathered in the casino for the Day 4 Championship match. A huge crowd amassed to watch from a section set up about ten feet outside the roped off area behind the table of play. Taking their seats, the Master of Ceremony (MC), speaking through a microphone, announced the names of the players along with a brief background, before explaining the rules for everyone to hear. The game had no bet limit and no time limit. When a player lost all his or her chips, that player was eliminated, and claimed the prize according to their placement.

To avoid a long drawn out game, the only rule change was for the remaining two players, regardless of their chip count, to have a one game winner-take-all showdown. The players shook their heads in affirmation of the rules, and the audience was ordered to remain completely quiet as a courtesy, to allow the contestants to focus on the game without distraction. Television feed of the game was sent to the bars to allow the patrons to watch while they enjoyed a cocktail.

Promptly at eight o'clock, the game began. In the first round, a small pot was won by Alex Manning after everyone else folded after the flop. Danny used the first three rounds of play to get a read on the other players. He picked up on a few hints during these rounds from Elainy Kazen and Bill Smith, who admitted after winning the second hand that he liked to play blind once in a while just to make the game more interesting. The sixth hand found Alex Manning and Bill Smith in a wild match. Smith played this hand blind. Danny and Christy, having poor hole cards, were not going to take any wild chances and immediately folded. Elainy Kazen looked at her hole cards and called the opening bet just to see the three cards from the flop. Seeing them she acted like she was going to fold her hand but decided to play. Smith pushed all his chips into the pot and said, "All In!"

Danny shook his head in disbelief as he winked at Christy who did the same and returned the wink. There being no sense trying to read someone who doesn't know what his hand is, Kazen turned her attention to Manning. Not picking up anything from him she thought for a few seconds before looking at her chips and loudly saying, "Call!" That brought a gasp from the crowd and a snicker from Danny. He saw what she did before she bet. So did Christy. Manning however, did not see that. The crowd quieted down and waited until Manning finished studying Kazen and said, "Call!" After all the bets were in, the players nervously turned over their cards, starting with Bill Smith. He turned over his mysterious blind hole cards, and much to his dismay, he had nothing but an Ace high card hand. Letting out a sigh of relief the other two players turned over their cards. Manning smiled as he showed a pair of Jacks. But his smile was short lived when Kazen revealed three deuces. That hand eliminated two players. Bill Smith and Alex Manning were listed as tied for fourth place. That didn't matter as the money for the last two places was the same; twenty five hundred dollars. Any elimination ties after that would be settled by a single elimination game with all cards dealt face up.

The next four hands played out fairly evenly with Danny having a slight edge as the chip leader. The fifth hand, Danny played his strategy perfectly. All three players had excellent hole cards. Kazen had the strongest hand through the flop with three aces. Christy needed one card for an outside straight and Danny needed one card for a flush. Dealing the Turn, or fourth community, card gave Christy the straight she needed. Danny could sense she had completed her hand. Kazen, still with three aces, bet 'All In' believing she held the best hand. Christy waited so as not to look too anxious. Then after looking at Kazen, then Danny, she said, "Call!" as she placed her chips into the pot. Seeing this Danny folded. This strategy put him in the final round as he was assured, after this hand; that the game was going to be down to him and one other player.

Both players turned up their cards. Christy saw the three Aces and knew all Kazen needed to win was either an Ace or a pair in the community cards. Everyone was quiet, and all eyes were on the dealer as he dealt the River, or fifth community card. It was an eight, and no help for Kazen's hand.

Christy let out a deep sigh as she won the round, and was going to play against Danny in a winner-take-all sudden death match to determine second place and the first place champion. Elainy Kazen smiled and congratulated both of them and wished them good luck as she walked away with third place, a five thousand dollar prize, and a nice round of applause from the audience. She was even more excited when she heard the whistling and cheering from Vicky and Stacie, which was actually meant for Christy and Danny. Danny thought, 'This couldn't have been better scripted if I did it myself.'

There was a five minute time out to allow the players a bathroom or a just a relaxing break. No one budged from the audience. Christy and Danny got up from their seats to get a drink of water before returning to the table where they gave each other a tight hug and wished each other the best as they waited to play. The dealer opened a fresh deck of cards, pulled out the jokers, and after retrieving the deck from the shuffling machine he wished them good luck before dealing the cards. To add a little more drama and excitement, Danny asked Christy, "How about we play this game Bill Smith style? Blind since it's either all face up or face down!" She laughed and said, "I thought you didn't like that style." Smiling he said, "Oh c'mon, it's Ok. Let's give the audience a little drama."

They requested the dealer to deal their hole cards face down. He smiled and agreed. Danny and Christy stood up with their hand around each other's waist and watched the cards. The flop showed a 2 of hearts, Jack of hearts, and a 5 of diamonds. The River card was an 8 of hearts and the Turn card was a 7 of hearts.

Laughing Christy said to Danny, "When you called playing blind, shit poker, you weren't kidding. Seeing this crap I agree." He laughed and replied, "Well, let's turn our cards over and see what we have. Ladies first?" She answered, "Ok mister!" Turning over her cards first, one of them was the 10 of diamonds. No help. Turning over the second card the audience let out a loud roar and cheered as she held it up for them to see. She smiled and said, "Queen of hearts! That's a Queen high flush for me. Beat that my man!" Danny smiled and said, "Well I'll give it my best shot. Here it goes!" The first card he turned over was an Ace of diamonds. No help.

Peeking at his second card before turning it over he then placed it back face down on the table and took a step back.

Nothing on his face gave any indication of his hand. He thought, 'Let's work the crowd.' He turned and addressed the crowd asking them, "How about if we wait until tomorrow morning before I show you?" This brought a round of laughter as well as some funny comments from the crowd. He said, "C'mon. Do you really want to see it?" The crowd responded with a resounding, "Yes! Yes!" It took about four seconds before they broke out into a chant of: "Show us! Show us! Show us!" Vicky said to Stacie, "That's my dad. He really knows how to work up a crowd. Whether he wins or loses they love him! *He won them over." Stacie replied, "He won me over with his first hello! The rest is gravy. Hey! Look at my mom!" Looking at Christy she was wearing a huge smile as she stood there, with her hands folded under her chin, laughing and enjoying the show he was putting on. Danny put his hands up and said, "Ok! Ok! Well. Here it is."*

Holding Christy around her waist he picked up the card and said, "Here you go honey. You look at it first and keep it to yourself." Seeing the card she laughed while covering her mouth with her hands. The crowd was quiet as they waited. Seeing Christy give him a kiss made them say, "Ahhh!" in unison. He let the dealer peek at his card before turning to the audience. The couple smiled and the crowd erupted as he turned it over and revealed the King of hearts! His King high flush won the tournament.

He took first place and the Championship along with the fifteen thousand dollar and future cruise for two, prizes. Christy took second place along with the ten thousand dollar prize. The MC had the winners line up for a picture and wave to the audience. He congratulated them on behalf of Atlantic Cruise Lines as the audience gave them a round of applause. Afterwards, the crowd was allowed to meet and speak with the finalists.

Vicky and Stacie were the first to get to them as they hugged Danny and Christy and high fived each other. As the people in the crowd were talking to the them Christy checked on the time. She thought, 'Oh my it's past eleven o'clock. I've got to get back to my room soon and get ready to meet Clint for the unveiling.' Thanking the others and excusing herself she turned to Danny and gave him a short kiss on his lips and a huge hug. Her nervous shaking told him everything. Then she let him go, stepped back, and looked at him. Her eyes were a little red and her bottom lip was beginning to quiver before she gave him a slight grin and told him before leaving, "I've got to go now. There's something I have to do, and it can't wait." He answered, "No problem. I'll see you for breakfast in the morning." After she left, he checked the time. Seeing that it was almost eleven fifteen p.m. he quickly walked over to Vicky.

His daughter winked at him and said, "It's getting late Prince Charming and your Cinderella is gonna be looking online for you." He laughed and said, "You know what to do. I'm going to my room. See you in a little while." Suddenly another voice from behind him said, "You mean see us in a little while, right Clint?" He turned and smiled, and before he could get a word out, Stacie grabbed him, hugged and squeezed him and with tears of happiness in her eyes she said, "Vicky told me while we were in the crowd. Why did you think the cheering was so loud? That was me! *This is just like a fairy tale come true! I promise I won't tell mom anything. I'll be as quiet as a church mouse and play my part. I'm so nervous!"*

He wiped her eyes for her, kissed her cheek, and said, "Thank you. And **it is** *like a storybook. I could not have written a better story so far. And I certainly could not have asked to be dealt a more perfect hand. She had the Queen of hearts and I had the King of hearts! Ok. Now I need you two to take your places. We're behind schedule. Hurry! Or this ship may turn into a pumpkin!" The young ladies gave him another hug before they left. He waited a couple more minutes while he talked with a few people before leaving for his cabin.*

Chapter 18
Pretty Cowgirl Finally Meets Clint

Walking *as fast as he could down to his cabin, Danny entered and quickly washed and groomed himself. Pulling out his tuxedo he changed clothes. He wanted to look his best for when, as he thought, 'Clint will now come out from behind his avatar to meet Pretty Cowgirl.' Checking the time, he took his phone and logged into the poker app and waited for her invitation.*

Meanwhile Vicky and Stacie worked as quickly as possible. Vicky arranged for thirty or so people to gather together in the section of the Lido Deck that had no ceiling, but rather an unobstructed open view of the sky, and an open view of the Majestic Deck above. Also on the Lido Deck was a DJ playing music every night until one a.m. Vicky gave him twenty dollars and he agreed to play the song she selected as soon as she requested it. He completely understood the situation. The rest of the crowd on the Lido Deck stayed after Vicky told them what was going on. Now there was an audience of almost fifty people waiting to witness the event. Vicky took her place with her camera behind the DJ and waited. Stacie called Vicky from her cabin and left her phone on as she was busy shadowing her mom. Vicky was listening on the other end so that she could message her dad. It was now eleven fifty p.m.

In her cabin Christy was getting anxious. Seeing the time she didn't want to wait too long so she decided to log onto the game. While she was doing this Stacie was laying on her bed pretending she was reading a book. All the while she had her phone line open with Vicky listening on the other end. Vicky's phone was muted to keep any noise from coming through Stacie's phone. Now logged on the game Christy was looking through her list of tagged friends. She stopped and smiled when she saw Clint online. She went through the motions of inviting him to a private table. Breathing deeply she waited for him to join her. Stacie glanced over at her mom every so often but kept her facial expressions and emotions concealed.

Receiving the invitation Danny heard his phone beep just as he finished dressing. He smiled in the mirror and said, "There she is. Ok. Let's do it!" Accepting her invitation took him to a private table where it was only the two of them. She typed, 'Hello my handsome Clint. My soon to be not mysterious man anymore. How are you tonight?' He replied, 'Hello my Pretty Cowgirl. I hope you're doing well. As for me well I'm a little nervous right now. How about you?' Shaking her head as she replied, 'I've got about a million butterflies in my stomach right now. Other than that I'm doing fine. I had a great day today. You see I'm out in the Caribbean on a cruise ship with my daughter and it's beautiful. Where are you?'

He laughed as he typed, "Right now I'm in my room. But it's such a beautiful night that I'm going to go outside and get some fresh air.' She smiled and typed, 'Yes. It's a beautiful night out here too. Plenty of stars out there along with a bright full moon. Well it's now twelve midnight and I guess we both know what that means.' Danny wrote, 'I sure do. Are you ready?' Christy nervously typed, 'I'm as ready as I'll ever be. Do you want to go first?' Danny replied, 'Sure. But first please give me a minute so I could get outside.'

Christy waited for him. Danny stood up, and opening his cabin door, he looked down the hallway towards her room to make sure the coast was clear. Then he made a swift exit to the stairwell and up the stairs. He continued walking to the Majestic Deck as he typed, 'Ok. Sorry for the delay. I'm outside and the sky is just as beautiful as you described it.' Walking over to the rail he saw Vicky waving to him from the Lido Deck below. He gave her the signal. She acknowledged it and told the crowd that everything was a go. She ducked behind the

DJ's large speaker and turned on the video camera. She put her phone up to her ear and waited for Stacie.

He read Pretty Cowgirl's reply without any delay. She wrote, 'Ok. I'm ready.' He messaged back, 'I've got a great idea. First before I change my avatar to a picture of me would you do something please? It would mean a lot to me.' She wrote, 'I guess so. What is it?' He wrote, 'I want you to do this. Please go outside and stand on the highest deck of the ship and focus only on the moon. Ok? This way we can feel a sense of being together while we're both watching it.' She thought, 'What a romantic idea!' and typed, 'That sounds so nice. I got chills just thinking about it. Ok. Give me a couple of minutes.' He typed back, 'Sure. Just let me know when you're there.'

Putting on her shoes she told her daughter she was going out for a little while. Stacie shook her head and returned to her pretend reading. Vicky listened and heard it all. When Christy left the room Stacie got up and listened at the door until she no longer heard her mom's footsteps. Talking into the phone she laughed and said, "Vicky. The eagle has taken off! I'll see you on the Lido Deck in three minutes. Hurrying, Stacie put on her shoes, and opening the door she left the room and took a different route to get to the Lido Deck where she took her place next to Vicky, who moved behind a large wooden stand behind the DJ and away from the loud speakers.

They had a perfect view of the open area on the Majestic Deck about twenty five feet away from them. Vicky's camera had a lens that could easily capture a clear high density picture from over thirty feet away. The stage was set and ready for action.

There she came. Christy walked gracefully up the steps from the Lido Deck and into perfect position on the top deck of the ship next to the railing that overlooked the Lido Deck below. Danny stood watching her from the farthest point at the back of the Majestic Deck in the darkest area he could find. She never noticed him. Now leaning against the rail she gazed at the moon as she held out her phone.

Messaging Clint she typed, 'Ok my man. I'm on the top deck and I'm looking at the moon.' Then he typed, 'Ok. Before I send you my picture I want to try something. Please play along. It will only take a minute. Ok?' She smiled and answered, 'Ok.' He typed, 'I want you to focus on the moon for about thirty seconds. Then I want you to close your eyes for one minute and imagine that you see me. Picture what you think I look like. There's an old superstition that believes, if you do this, then after you open your eyes you will see your true love in the moonlight. Try it and tell me when you're going to start, and I will do the same thing. And when we both open our eyes, we should see each other. I heard it works every time.' She laughed as she messaged, 'You're really something else. Ok. I'll try it. As soon as you message me back 'Go'.

Danny typed the word 'Go' and sent it. Watching her from behind he saw her look up at the moon. That was his signal to alert Vicky to get the crowd noise up. Seeing this Vicky signaled to the crowd to get louder. The DJ helped by raising the volume of the reggae music he was playing. This gave Danny the chance to quietly walk up behind Christy. After counting forty five seconds Danny stopped about ten feet behind her and waited. With her back to him and the loudness coming from the deck below her, she never detected his presence. Waiting for her to open her eyes and send a message to Clint, he stood there nervously holding his cell phone in front of him. When she finally opened her eyes she stared at the moon for a few seconds before replying.

She typed, 'Ok. I've done what you asked. It was a romantically beautiful sentiment. And yes. I saw the face of my true love in the moonlight. Did you see the face of your true love too?' She sent the message and then continued to stare at the moon. Danny read it and messaged back, 'Yes I did. I saw just what I've imagined all along. Now I'll ask you to do one last thing and I promise it will be good.' She grinned as she messaged, 'Ok. One last thing. Then show me and tell me who you are.'

Danny nervously typed and sent the message, 'This is a very powerful thing we both did by looking at the moon and wishing and dreaming. I know it worked because if you turn around you'll see the man that was revealed to you in the moonlight. Do it. He's standing there waiting and his heart is now beating only for you!'

Smiling and playing along she thought, 'Ok.' Turning around and seeing Danny standing there sent shock waves through her and made her entire body weak. Her eyes widened and her jaw dropped. She thought it was her mind playing tricks on her. She couldn't believe her eyes! She stood there in awe as he tapped his phone once. The vibration from her cell phone snapped her out of her state of shock. It was a message from Clint that read, 'It's really me.....Danny....my Pretty Cowgirl and I'm so glad it's you Christy!'

Her surprise and excitement made her heart pound like a sledgehammer as her lips pursed and her eyes filled up with tears. Her breathing was shallow and fast as if she was hyperventilating. Almost frozen from shock and disbelief she dropped her cell phone. Staring at the entire scene from below Stacie was now balling her eyes out as she watched a beautiful love story unfolding before her as Danny and her mom stood there lost in their defining moment. Vicky couldn't hold in her reaction either and signaling to the DJ he immediately played the soft slow beautiful love song that they danced to while at one of the clubs one night during the cruise titled, 'You And I'. The crowd saw this and moved closer to watch. Most of them with their eyes and mouths wide open. It was as if they were watching a fairy tale coming to life.

Christy blinked several times thinking she was still seeing a picture in her mind. She asked, "Clint? Danny?" He answered, "Yes Christy my Pretty Cowgirl it's me. One and the same." She asked, "How did you know?"

He walked to her, took her by the hand and said, "My little sister found out from your little sister about Clint." Tears fell from her eyes as she looked at him, and putting her arms around him she said, "You were right about the moon. You were the picture I had in my mind for that minute and the picture I had since I first laid eyes on you. I wanted it to be you so bad that I didn't want to open my eyes ever again." They embraced and passionately kissed as the music played and everyone from the Lido Deck applauded, cheered, and whistled.

After their kiss Christy stared into Danny's eyes and said, "I can't believe this is happening to me. I wanted this so bad. It was even in our final cards at the tournament. Remember? We were dealt the King and Queen of hearts." Now laughing through her tears she asked, "You didn't tell the dealer about this, did you?" Holding her, Danny laughed and said, "He must have known something! Maybe he looked at the moon before dealing that last hand! I also wanted this so bad. And if you can't believe it then look down there behind the bar at who's waving at us. The whole thing is being videoed."

She said, "Ahhh, those two little stinkers. They really are matchmakers! Well? What do we do now?" Danny wiped her eyes and said, "I don't know about you but I told my family what I would do if Pretty Cowgirl turned out to be exactly what I was hoping she would be!" She asked, "What's that?" Danny answered, "You see, when I found out about you two days ago, I visited that jewelry store across from the piano bar and got you this."

The crowd erupted in cheers and applause, while Vicky and Stacie were hugging each other, still crying tears of joy and jumping up and down when they saw Danny hold Christy's hand, drop to one knee, and propose. More tears of joy poured out of Christy as she accepted. Trembling with excitement she let out a loud scream before shouting "YES!" Danny stood up and hugged her as tight as he could. It was the fulfilling feeling in their hearts that they both searched for and finally found it in each other. They held each other tightly and passionately kissed several times.

Both of them were trembling with joy and the excitement of the moment and the satisfaction they felt *knowing they were blessed with another chance at true love. They held each other like they were never going to let go. Christy dried her eyes and said, "That song is perfect. Like our first date when I asked you to join me for breakfast at nine o'clock just...you and I. Then you repeated that to me; just...you and I." Danny replied, "I remember. When you said that it made my heart skip a beat. It's what I wanted when I first saw you and what I wanted when I imagined who you were when we played online. When you and I were on that private island in my mind. Yes my love just....you and I."*

With their eyes closed they continued holding each other. Christy chuckling through her tears of joy said, "That was a great way of setting up Clint's unveiling. I'm glad you used that story about the moon. It was so romantic. I'll never forget it. I'm still in shock. If it wasn't for the reality of all the kissing and hugging we did, I would have thought it was all just a dream." Danny smiled and replied, "I needed that as much as you and even though I found out that you were my Pretty Cowgirl, I still had such a difficult time believing it. I wanted to rush to your room and tell you but I felt it would be better some other way. So I came up with the moon story and you and our girls played your parts perfectly."

Christy's lips trembled as she pulled him in for another passionate kiss. Then hugging him she whispered in his ear, "I want to make love to you tonight. I can't wait." Danny pressed her tighter against him and they both laughed when he said, "Me too just...you and I!" He continued, "But first we have to go downstairs. We have two very excited young ladies bursting at the seams waiting to congratulate and maul us. I also have some champagne on ice reserved for all of us."

Christy sarcastically replied as she stood back and held Danny's hands, "They can wait...can't they? Hahaha!" He responded, "Yeah. Why don't we let them dangle in suspense for a while. We can go down to my room through the elevator from this floor." Staring at their daughters he laughed and said, "C'mon. Let's go see them, get some champagne, and then go to my room and share the first of many passionate love making nights together." Christy answered as she waved to the young ladies below, "It's a deal. Oh by the way, I just thought of something so great and so funny." Danny asked, "What's that?" She answered, "I got my wish! Earlier I wished that I could have you and Clint and thought how that was such a terrible thing to have two men." He answered, "That is *funny because I thought the same thing about you and Pretty Cowgirl. We both got our wish. That moon is a powerful force. And I'm so in love with you and I can't believe we first actually got to know each other while we were total strangers."*

Breaking their embrace the couple turned and walked hand in hand down the steps to the Lido Deck where they were joined by Vicky and Stacie. The young ladies cried tears of joy as they hugged and kissed the newly engaged couple. Despite only knowing each other for a few days, they acted like they were a family that had been together for years. Wiping their eyes they held onto Danny and Christy tightly.

Stacie was overjoyed knowing she was going to have a new dad that she was already in love with. And Vicky shared the same sentiments towards having Christy as her future mom. Both young ladies were already best of friends and now they were delighted that they were going to be sisters. Stacie's bonus was going to be a whole new family including two brothers, another sister, and two nephews. They all laughed when Stacie realized something and said, "Well mom. How does it feel to know that you'll also be a young grandma?" Christy smiled and answered, "I'm looking forward to it."

Then Vicky spoke up and sarcastically asked, "Dad? Whatever happened to your 'I'm gonna take a relationship really slow thing?' I know you told us at the table that day what you were going to do if Pretty Cowgirl turned out to be who you imagined. But your proposal probably shocked me more than it shocked Christy!" Danny smiled and said, "Honey? After finding out who my Pretty Cowgirl was...this was as slow as I could go!" They all laughed and continued to laugh when

Christy added, "After I found out that you were Clint, if you didn't propose to me...I was gonna propose to you!"

All four of them waved and thanked the crowd as they walked to the elevator and took it down to the night club on the Promenade Deck where Danny had champagne on ice waiting for them to toast to the occasion. Afterwards, Christy went to her room and packed her night gown along with a change of clothes and took them with her to Danny's room for the first of many nights of romance and passion.

Vicky and Stacie smiled and high fived each other as they walked by Danny's cabin and saw the 'Do Not Disturb' sign hooked around the door handle. Stacie said, "You know. I couldn't have wished for a better dad and a better sister! And I thought my mom was never ever gonna find happiness again." Vicky responded, "Same here. For a while there it looked like he was gonna give up! I'm so glad that I'm going to have someone in my life again like Christy along with a new best friend and sister too!"

Chapter 19
A New Story Begins

Hearing *the news, Danny's family could not believe it. Not only that his fantasy woman turned out to be someone on the cruise but that he actually proposed marriage right on the spot just like he said he would. The board of directors at the bank even took an interest in this amazing story, and published a feature article in the personal section of its monthly newsletter. Christy and Stacie made many trips to Charlotte to spend time with Danny and got to know their future extended family very well. They spent time with Chris and Donna as well as Stephen and the children. Sunday family get-togethers were now more exciting and fun when Christy and Stacie attended.*

It was not going to be long before they joined Danny in Charlotte permanently. Likewise, Danny made many trips to Orlando to stay and visit with Christy and her family. Many of whom lived in the small surrounding towns of Eustis, Umatilla, Paisley, and others. Love grew stronger between them and they spent every passionate night they could together. Stacie's relationship with Danny grew stronger as well. She took him out a few times in Orlando so she could show off her future older brother, as she referred to him, to her friends. Life was now better than any of them expected.

Danny and Christy planned to get married after she and Stacie moved to Charlotte, North Carolina. As far as work was concerned, It was an easy transfer from region to region for Christy, while Vicky had no problem finding a position for Stacie in the hospital. With so many openings she found a great position in Pediatrics that she loved better than the one she had in Orlando.

Within four months after moving in with Danny they were married. It was a beautiful church wedding. The kind of ceremony you'd imagine that was performed when royalty married. Their ceremony included a traditional ritual they borrowed from the Greek Orthodox weddings where crowns are placed on the bride and groom during the ceremony signifying them as the King and Queen of their home. The couple had the crowns adorned with hearts. Stacie was the Maid of Honor while Chris was the Best Man. Christy's father flew up from Florida to walk her down the aisle for the second time. There were four sets of ushers and bridesmaids.

The reception was in the large room at the country club where Danny held a membership. Nearly three hundred guests attended including all their family and friends. There was gourmet food served buffet style, an open bar, and a DJ who played non-stop dance music, including 'You And I,' which was the first song they danced to as husband and wife.

Guests came by to congratulate the newlyweds while they sat at the wedding party's table. There they met some people for the first time. Others were friends from Florida and North Carolina. Danny and Christy mingled and spoke with all their guests.

One time Danny found it very surprising and amusing when Vicky winked at her dad as a friend of his walked up to them. Danny smiled and said, "Well hello Fred. So glad you could make it." Turning to introduce Christy he said, "Honey. This is Fred. He's a colleague of mine from the bank." She shook his hand and said, "It's very nice to meet you Fred." Danny said to Fred, "I don't see Maxine. Is she here?" Fred answered, "Well no. You see Maxine and I are getting a divorce." Danny said, "Fred I'm sorry. I didn't know." Fred smiled and said, "That's OK. I'm perfectly fine." Now whispering to Danny he said, "I caught her with another man...again! This time I got pictures. Well I had enough and told her to leave, and I immediately filed for divorce with my attorney. I feel so much better. As a matter of fact I'm *here with my date. I'll go get her and bring her here to meet you. You'll never guess who it is!"*

Coming back within about a minute Fred caught Danny's attention and said, "Hey Danny. I'd like to introduce you to my date." Danny's eyes almost popped out of his head as he beat Fred to the punch. Surprised he said, "Simone!" Extending a hand Simone said, "We meet again Danny." After shaking his hand Simone smiled, winked, then turned and walked away.

Fred looked at Danny and shrugging his shoulders he said, "What can I tell you? After all Maxine put me through, I needed a friend. That's all we are. Just friends. I met Simone on a dating site. She's amazing. Come to find out we knew each other from the bank." Danny's jaw dropped as Fred walked away. Christy asked, "What's wrong dear." Looking around he saw Vicky holding her stomach and laughing hysterically along with Stephen and Chris. Shaking his head at them he then turned to Christy and said, "Honey. I'll tell you some other time. Let's just say that I'm so glad you are all that you are and more than I ever imagined, and I love you so much." She smiled and said, "I love you too dear and I still can't believe that we're so fortunate to have two chapters in our fairy tale book."

Using the cruise Danny won in the tournament for part of their honeymoon, the couple was gone for almost three weeks. Along with their cruise they spent one week in Greece and another in Italy. They once again resumed living the life of King and Queen of their home.

The last we see of Christy and Danny is both of them standing embraced in front of their living room fireplace. On the wall over the mantle now are three pictures. To the right is the wedding picture of Danny and Rachel. To the left is the wedding picture of Christy and John. And in the center is the picture the photographer took of them silhouetted in front of the beautiful sunrise on the cruise ship where they first met. Their wedding picture was hanging on their bedroom wall. Their next fairy tale story had just begun.

The End

Made in the USA
Columbia, SC
30 May 2024

36060452R00128